Dibidalen

ten stories

Dibidalen

ten stories

SEÁN VIRGO

thistledown press

Thistledown Press Ltd.
118 - 20th Street West
Saskatoon, Saskatchewan, S7M 0W6
www.thistledownpress.com

Library and Archives Canada Cataloguing in Publication

Virgo, Seán, 1940-
Dibidalen / Seán Virgo.

Short stories.
Issued also in an electronic format.
ISBN 978-1-927068-06-9

I. Title.
PS8593.I72D53 2012 C813'.54 C2012-904712-0

Cover painting, *Tobias and the Archangel Raphael returning with the Fish* after Adam Elsheimer (c1574-1610). Oil on copper.
©National Gallery, London/ Art Resource, NY
Cover and book design by Jackie Forrie
Printed and bound in Canada

Canada Council for the Arts Conseil des Arts du Canada

Canadian Heritage Patrimoine canadien

Thistledown Press gratefully acknowledges the financial assistance of the Canada Council for the Arts, the Saskatchewan Arts Board, and the Government of Canada through the Canada Book Fund for its publishing program.

Dibidalen

ten stories

for Moya

Sleep deep, little sister –
remember us in your dreams.

Contents

"L'autre monde n'est plus pas étanche qu'est une barque."

— Pascal Quignard, *Tous Les Matins Du Monde*

Before Ago

A stranger came to the poor man's door.

I need a boy to come with me on my journey.

My son is lazy. He is good for nothing.

The better for me and the worse for him.

So they left the village and went across the valley.

The boy was tired. He was hungry and thirsty.

I cannot go any further.

The stranger beat him with his stick.

They climbed to the edge of the valley.

The boy fell to the ground.

I cannot go on.

The Cat can have you then.

The sun was going down. With the shadows came the cry of the Cat.

The boy saw the stranger, far away, very small.

He ran and ran till he came up to him. He fell at his feet.

There was a pool of water there.

The stranger gave him some food, a little.

The boy slept.

The sun was coming up. With the shadows came the cry of the Cat.

The boy saw the stranger, far away, very small.

There was desert between them.

The boy began to run. He heard the snakes singing among the stones. He jumped over a grease bush and a snake bit him on the heel.

He ran and ran and fell at the stranger's feet.

The stranger beat him with the stick and they went on.

The boy's foot began to swell. It was hard for him to walk.

I will wait for you at the river.

When the boy reached the river, the stranger was on the far bank. He had a fire and was cooking a trout. The scent came across the water.

He waved for the boy to come to him.

I am afraid of water. I cannot swim over.

The stranger turned the fish on his stick. The scent was so good.

The sun was going down. With the shadows came the cry of the Cat.

The boy went into the river. The water came over his head.

There was moonlight in the river. The fishes were singing their songs.

The boy walked across the riverbed, and a black fish came and bit him below the knee.

When he came out of the river it was daylight. He fell at the stranger's feet.

Let me sleep now.

Will you give me your songs?

The boy's head was full of the song of the snakes, like dry seeds on a drum. It was full of the song of the fishes, like wind in the treetops.

But he could not sing.

The stranger beat him with the stick and they went on.

The boy's leg was swollen, it was hard for him to walk.

I will wait for you at the cliff.

When the boy reached the cliff, the stranger was down below. He had a fire and was cooking a partridge. The scent came up over the rocks.

He waved for the boy to come to him.

I am afraid of heights. I cannot climb down.

The stranger turned the partridge on his stick. The scent was so good.

The sun was going down. With the shadows came the cry of the Cat.

The boy climbed over the cliff's edge. His leg was swollen, it pulled him down. He fell onto a ledge.

It was dark on the cliff. And there was a bad smell. It was his leg. It smelled of rotting meat.

Something cut him in the darkness. There were small voices, singing, and his thigh was being cut, and cut.

When the day came he saw that he was in an eagle's nest. The young eagles were pecking his thigh.

He fell again. His leg was swollen, it broke his fall. He lay at the stranger's feet.

I cannot go any further.
There is not far to go.

The stranger took him up on his back. He carried him through the forest, and into a valley.

There was a village below them. It was like the one he had left behind.

Will you give me your songs?

The boy's head was full of the song of the snakes, like dry seeds on a drum. It was full of the song of the fishes, like wind in the treetops.

It was full of the song of the eagles, like green wood in a fire.

But he could not sing.

Keep them for yourself then.

The stranger gave him his stick. It was light as a reed and hard as a bone. It had its own song.

The boy went down to the village. People held their noses. First they laughed at him, then they threw stones.

At the end of the day they closed up all the houses.

The sun was going down. With the shadows came the cry of the Cat.

The boy stood outside the village, leaning on his stick. And the Cat came out of the shadows.

The boy's shit ran down his leg. He could not move.

The Cat walked around him. Its cry filled the valley.

The boy lifted his stick, and the Cat pounced.

It took the leg in its jaws. It swallowed the poison.

The leg became whole again. The Cat lay dead at the boy's feet.

The boy started singing. He sang the eagles' song, and the fishes', and the snakes'. He beat the stick on the ground, and it sang with him.

He sat beside the body of the Cat, and listened. All night he heard the songs of the dreaming people, safe in their houses.

The sun was coming up, and with the shadows came the cry of the Cat. It came from the boy's own mouth.

He went down to the village. He looked for the poorest home.

He beat on the door with his stick.

I need a man to come with me on my journey.

My husband is afraid of his own hand's shadow.

The better for me said the boy *and the worse for him.*

Eggs in a Field

There was a man found eggs in a field.

One, two and three, the colour of stones in a pool.

Two he took for himself, and walked on from the place, but he let one fall from his hand as he leapt the stile and he came back again for the third.

He went on through the gap in the hill and when he came to his house —

The roses by the wall were white that had been yellow as quinces.

The smoke lay over his chimney like a great bag of meal.

It was a cross dog met him at the gate and would not let him by.

The woman at the door in his wife's own dress was like no one he knew, and the child in her arms turned its face from him.

"We've no call for strangers here," said the woman

"It's yourself is the stranger then," said the man, "from where I'm standing."

"Then stand no longer," said the woman, "and be done with frightening the child." And she took herself into the house.

The man looked at the dog and saw no good in it. And he went back the road that he came, looking to find his way.

He came through the gap in the hill, and the way that he found went along by the gate to the field.

The cock bird sat on an ash branch. It filled the air with its rage –

"My house is broken," it sang.
"Bad luck to the thief till the last day.
"May the shame of it break him in two."

"Is it only for the eggs, then?" said the man. "I have them with me yet, still warm in my hand. Point me the place, now, and I'll bring them home again."

"What's lost is gone forever," sang the cock bird, but it flew out over the field and the man followed after.

The hen bird ran in the grass. She cried her heartful upon him –

"My hope is stolen from me. My care is broken.
"Let the thief go alone through the empty world,
"And the bad heart within him."

"Be easy and let that alone now," said the man. "I have troubles of my own this day." And he found the place and set the two eggs down where they'd lain before.

"What's lost is found now," he said. "I meant you no harm."

And he went as before to the stile, with the birds crying after him, and on through the gap in the hill and into the boreen that ran the back way to his house.

He walked for an hour, and he walked for two, but he saw no end to the boreen, and now the sun was ahead of him, and now it was behind. "It's fairy-led I am surely," said the man, and he minded his grandmother's words. He took off his coat so, and put in his arms through the sleeves, front to back, and turned three times about on his shadow and three times back again, and there was his dog coming up the boreen to meet him, and the way clear.

When they came to his house —

There was a yellow rose by the wall for every
white one that grew there.

The smoke went up from his chimney and twirled
in the wind.

The child was out playing by the well.

But the woman under the apple tree in his wife's own dress was like no one he knew.

"You've no dog with you now," said the man, "to keep
me from my own."

"If the dog will come in, and the child will go out,"
said the woman, "I will give you welcome,
whoever you may be."

But the dog would not go in at the gate, and the child began crying in fright and ran to the woman's side.

"There'll be no welcome here," said the woman, "for man or beast that puts fear in a child." And she took herself and the child back in at the door.

The man looked at the dog, and had no word to say, and he went back up the boreen with the dog at his heel, looking to find his way.

They came through the gap in the hill, and the way that they found led along by the ditch of the field.

The cock bird sat on a thorn bush. It sang till the branches shook –

"Too late for the mending," it sang.
"Too late for returning.
"Too late for the broken home and the child lost
forever."

"I am asking your help," said the man, "whatever the price of it. Will you help me to find my way?"

The hen bird ran in the grass. She cried till the rushes took up her song:

"Oh, oh, oh, see where she lies," they sang.
"Oh, oh, oh, see where the hound has its teeth in her."

And when the man looked, there was his dog by the stile, lapping the egg that was spilt in the grass, and the glair of it dripping from its snout.

"Ach now," said the man. "What would you have me do? 'Tis beyond any help and indeed I am sorry for it."

"'Tis the thief's own child that is eaten there now,"
sang the cock bird.
"He has broken his own heart so," cried the hen bird
in the grass.

The man fell into a rage and a dread then. He leapt over the stile and went back through the gap in the hill, kicking badgers out of his heels, and on down the boreen. And when he came to his house –

There were brambles upon the wall where the
roses had grown.
The chimney was cold, and the thatch fallen in at
the gable end,

and the nettles grew thick about the step.

An old woman was grubbing roots from the earth around the well.

The man stood by the broken gate. "Do you know me at all?" he called to her.

The woman stood up and rested her hand on the well's lip. "How would I know you," she said, "and myself all alone in this place these thirty years?"

The man's heart turned cold in his breast and the sun went out of the sky.

He turned away from the gate and went up the dark boreen, and there was his dog at the head of it waiting, and the night bird calling.

They came through the gap in the hill, himself and the dog, looking to find their way.

And the way that they found leads along by every man's house.

And now the moon is ahead of them, and now it is behind.

The Shark Mother

There was a boy who was born by a river where ships came in from every place in the world. When he grew older he went down after school to the quays where the sailors gathered and threw dice and waited for the tide to turn. He ran errands for them and brought them the news of the town, and one day a brown winking man with eyes as pale as a sea bird's whispered the words that he longed above all things to hear.

He went back to his house, and pulled out his father's old sea chest from under the stair, and dried his mother's tears.

That night he stood on a ship's deck and watched as the lights of the town disappeared and the river gave way to the sea; and he breathed that salt air for the next forty years, growing to manhood and becoming in turn a boatswain, a mate, and at last the master of his own tall ship, sailing the Seven Seas.

The sea of gold and silver, where the sirens
conjured the winds.
The sea of furs and amber, where the great whale
fishes blew.
The sea of nutmegs and parrots and cloves.
The sea of rubies and peacocks and tea.
The sea of apes and ivory, where the slaves cried
out in the hold.
The sea of silk and china and pearls, where the
pirates haunted the bays.
And the ancient sea at the heart of them all, where
the trade routes began and ended.

He came back each year to the river where he began, and each year he passed a green headland with a lighthouse beacon, and a long spit of sand that sheltered the harbour below. Gulls hung on the wind above the white church on the hillside, and sheep dotted the bracken slopes behind the houses. He told himself he would make his home there someday, when he was done with the sea.

In the year that his mother died, he sailed far to the south and west, through a chain of islands where palm trees leaned over the strands, and there one night, lying at anchor on a dark lagoon, he watched men carrying torches out over the water while women sang and danced on the reef, calling the bonito fish in to the nets. And a girl rose laughing beside his ship, waist-deep in the foam, her teeth gleaming in the torchlight.

He came back that way, on his voyage home, and searched through the islands until he found her. He brought her away with him, back to the river of his birth, and sold his ship and bought a house in the town on the green headland, and became the harbour master there. And there their son was born.

The boy grew up in a silent house. His father seemed a different person at home from the man who took him sometimes to the excise house down at the harbour, or to the tavern beside it. There, among sailors and fishermen, with his traveller's tales and shanty songs, he was full of quick jests and laughter, but as they walked back through the town his steps grew heavier and gloom settled over his face. They ate their meals in silence, and the boy's mother never sat with them.

She moved like a shadow through the house, with timid eyes and downturned mouth, but her touch was the softest thing in the world, and her goodnight kiss closed his eyes into deep green dreams from which he woke in the darkness, wishing he could remember.

Every day she walked out alone, beyond the town, but some afternoons she would wait for him in the lane behind the school and they would go hunting together.

There were trails in the bracken coombes where she set snares for the rabbits, but most often they went to the rivermouth past the spit and there he would wade knee deep in the stream, driving the fishes towards her darting hands. She would split a fish open with her thumbnail, and share the sweet strips of meat that lay under the fins.

Those were happy times, but most afternoons she wandered on her own, along the shore or out on the spit, and he could be alone in the house for an hour with his secrets.

On his tenth birthday he had climbed up into the roof, where a swallow was beating her wings in fright among the rafters. He caught the bird in his hands, and set her free through a gap in the tiles, and then behind the chimney he found the old sea chest with its great rusty lock.

From that day forward, whenever he was sad — when the fog crept in from the sea, or when the boys of the town were unkind to him after school — he would go up to his room, and climb through the hatchway into the roof, and sit beside the old chest and dream his dreams.

More and more the attic became for him the cabin his father had sailed in around the world, and the little gap in the tiles was a porthole that looked out on the Seven Seas. The gulls floating by the house were frigate birds and albatrosses, and the wind was the sea rushing by, or the surf on an island shore. Then he would hear his mother, quietly closing the back door below, and he'd listen, as he knew she was listening, for his father's steps in the lane outside, and then he would climb back down and leave his secrets behind.

But one summer day, when the attic was hot and sleepy, he pulled the sea chest out from the shadows and the hasp of the rusty lock came away in his hands. The lid fell open and there inside was a roll of white skin, the softest leather. Its smell was the smell left behind by the dreams he could never remember. But when he took hold of it he cried out in pain, for the underside of the skin was harsh as iron, and it stung him. Blood sprang from his middle finger, and when he put it to his mouth an icy chill filled his body. The air seemed too hot to breathe, the floor seemed to tip away, the rafters went round and round. He climbed down to his room and knelt by the open window, for his skin was on fire and the breeze that came up off the sea was gentle and cool.

There he stayed until he was called down to supper. But the smell of the rabbit stew that was waiting on his plate was more than he could bear. "The boy has a fever," his father said, and he carried him upstairs to bed. His mother bathed his face and chest with cold water, and stayed with him for an hour, but when she kissed him goodnight there was a question in her eyes that he did not know how to answer.

The room grew dark and the house fell quiet, and still his skin was burning. The sheets were a torment to him, the pillow scratched at his face. He wondered if he was dying. He longed for his mother's hands, spreading cool water across his skin, and the fever sang in his ears. "Leave your bed," said the fever, "and go to the open window." He went and looked out, and the night was full of stars, and the smell of the open sea.

"Take the skin," said his fever. "Take the white skin and go down to the shore."

"I have no strength to do that," cried the boy.

But the fever said, "The little waves will heal you."

So the boy climbed into the roof, and took the skin, and went down through the house. When he passed the room where his parents lay, his mother cried out and sat up staring. But she was deep in her dreams, and fell back again on the pillow.

The boy went out through the sleeping town. Not a light was burning, no dogs ran out from the doorways, and the old moon came up to meet him at the end of the street. She lighted his barefoot way, over the cobblestones and down the long hill above the harbour, out onto the sands.

The air was cold now, but his skin was still burning, and the further he walked along the spit, the heavier the white skin grew in his arms. He let it fall at last, at the water's edge, and it unrolled down the sloping sand. The dark side of the skin lay in the moonlight beside his shadow, in the shape of a great fish, with its head just touching the water.

And as he watched, a little wave came and slipped under the skin, and then another, so that the skin began floating away from the shore. Then a third little wave came and covered the boy's feet, and he knew that his fever had not lied. For the burning left him, wherever the little waves touched him, and he waded out from the sand till the water covered his knees, and then his waist, and the fever grew weaker and weaker.

His nightshirt floated around him, and the little waves tugged it and drew it down out of sight, and the boy took two more steps away from the shore. Beside him the dark skin floated, and he put out his hand to hold it and steady himself, for the sand was beginning to shift beneath his feet. Only his face was burning now. He dipped it into the water, and the little waves came playing in his ears, and the fever left him.

Then a big wave came surging and lifted him off his feet, and the dark skin wrapped itself around him, soft and strong as his mother's arms, and he breathed in the sea.

He could see the moonlight, through the fish's eyes, shining down through the water, and all at once he knew his way, for this was the place that he visited in his dreams, with the sounds and the perfumes of all the Seven Seas.

And he swam out, under the old moon's path on the waters, leaving his memories behind.

The Scapegoat

A man knelt down to drink in the forest.
He had killed a wolf, and skinned it, and his only thought now was to find his way home to the village.
He had followed the blood trail for a day and a half, across two low valleys, to a part of the forest he had never seen before.

The trees grew further apart here, and sunlight came down through the leaves above the stream.
He cleaned his hands, and drank from them. When the ripples faded, his face looked back at him from the water.
There was a bright stone on the stream's bed below his reflection, and when he picked it out from the gravel he knew, by its weight, that it was gold. He found another, and then another.

They were smooth but wrinkled, like small, unborn animals, and as he turned them on his palm, he heard the far off crying of dogs.

There was fear in the sound.
He felt as his wolf may have felt, though he did not know why.

He went up the stream with his bag and his bow, and hid by some rocks where the water tumbled into a pool.
He crouched there and listened to the sound of the dogs coming closer.
He could see gold gleaming everywhere on the floor of the pool.

The barking stopped. The echoes faded to nothing.

He sat very still, as though he were moss on the stones.
His eyes were closed, and the only sounds were the water's voice and his own heart beating.

When he looked up at last, three brindled dogs were standing over him.
They had thick leather collars, and their leashes trailed beside them.
The men followed after, in a line through the trees.
Their arrows were aimed at his breast.

They had tight lips and nostrils, and their eyes were paler than the sky.
They bound his arms behind him and led him away, down a long hillside with the dogs running on ahead.
It was nightfall before they stopped.

There was a fire burning, and other men standing around it.
They untied his arms, and one of them took his hand and sat down with him by the fire.
He was given fresh bread with a salty crust, and a speckled cheese that crumbled in his mouth. There was a sweet drink, too, passed from hand to hand in a jug that seemed carved out of stone. It smelled of honey and brought the blood up into his cheeks.

They watched him, without ever meeting his eyes.
Their voices were like the murmuring of wood doves.
He could make nothing of their words.

They paid no heed when he went to relieve himself, but the three dogs followed him through the trees, and waited until he came back to the fire.
One of them lay at his feet for the rest of the night, growling softly whenever he stirred.

He woke from a dream where he crouched by the waterfall, and the men and their dogs passed by without seeing him.
The wolf came down to drink at the pool, and looked over at him with pale, searching eyes.
There were fish in the depths of the pool, feeding upon the gold.
One by one, the bright stones were disappearing.
Then he remembered where he was.

He was wet with dew, and there was wind in the treetops like a stream rushing overhead.

In the half-light of dawn the men were shadows in the clearing.
They gave him water, and then bound his arms again and hurried him off down a trail as the sky lightened before them.

The dogs ran ahead, barking wildly.
A cart with high wheels was standing at the mouth of the trail.
A young boy sat astride the horse, turning to watch as he was hoisted into the cart.
Two of the men sat beside him as the cart moved away.

The forest changed as the morning wore on.
The trees became strangers, with thin branches and fluttering leaves, and the underbrush crowded beneath them.
The wind turned around. It seemed to die down, but then it came all at once in their faces, smelling of tinder, dust-laden.
Just as suddenly, it was gone. The cart wheels moaned over the rough trail. He ached in his bones.

They stopped only once in the day, and before they went on, the men tied a blue cloth tightly around his eyes.
Soon after, he felt the sun's heat, full and fierce on his face, and he knew he was outside the forest for the first time in his life.

It was dark when they took off the blindfold, and let him climb down.

He lay on his back in dry grass. The earth was still warm, and the air was mysterious with faint, mingled scents.
More stars than he'd ever imagined filled an endless sky.
Insects pulsed in the darkness; a fox barked; far away there were wolves.
But the silence was huge, all around him.

He could not guess how much time had passed.
The boy was tugging at his shoulder, a dark shape against the stars.
He was lifted back into the cart, his eyes covered again, his wrists bound together.

The sun's warmth told him when day came, but the voice of the wheels was his only guide.
They whispered and hissed through long grass till the sun was high.
They clattered across the stones of a dry stream bed and out onto sand, firm at first, then deep and heavy.
The wheels groaned into silence.
The men got down, and the boy was crying out at the horse. The wheels shuddered and heaved, and crept forward again.
Then there was hard-packed earth, and other wheels answering.

A clamour of hoofbeats and wheels broke around him.
There were voices there too, high and low, the queer dove-calling, whole families.

He felt the invisible stares as they passed, and he
yearned for the forest.

He closed his eyes, behind the blindfold, against the
tears.

There was a place in the shade of the alders, where the
water moved slow, and the trout on warm evenings
hung motionless over the stones.
He unrolled the snare from his wrist, the twine of his
wife's own hair, and let it down through the tree roots
into the stream.
The perfect stillness, his breath as steady as the fish's
below him, its gills closing and opening, the snare
easing upstream towards it.
Now the noose was over the tail, just wide enough to
clear the trout's body, the tremoring fins.
The slightest lift and it slid past the back fin, almost to
the gills.
Then the strike.

The fish was in the air, close to his face, its bright,
stippled flank, its golden eye.
And he was loping back down the deer trail, skirting
the marshes, the smoke from the houses greeting him
through the willows.

His cry of gladness became sorrow.

The hoofbeats and wheels were above and beside him,
sudden and close, as if they had entered a cave.

Then the wheels were on stone, and the echoes trailed alongside.
He guessed they were in a rock-cleft. He imagined dark cliffs.
The echoes fell back and merged with the growl of a storm.
There was sun on his face. The wheels stopped turning.

When they lifted him down, his legs failed. He fell on his knees and pitched forward, striking his head on the ground.
They held him under his arms and urged him forward, stepping blind across stone that was flat as ice on a pond.
He felt the quick tug of a knife as they set his arms free.
They pressed down on his shoulders. He was sitting.
A cold stone bench.
The blindfold was torn away.

He covered his eyes. He was pummelled by light and space.
It was a place from the stories he had never thought of believing.

Wherever he looked there were straight lines, dizzying.
The ground all around him was flat squares of stone, their edges touching. The lines sped away in a pattern that filled him with terror.
At the edge of the clearing were houses taller than the forest. They had the same pale sheen as the stones that covered the ground, and they threw no shadows.

Everything was stone, as though whole cliffs had been
hacked out and then built up again.
The earth was trembling.

Wagons and carts and a throng of people streamed on
either side, past the houses.
The stone walls hurled out their noise through the
clearing.
The voice of the storm.

Before him the clearing stretched away, further and
straighter than any reach of the river.
The low sun was turning the most distant houses blood
red.
Five backlit figures were watching him.

The tallest came close and stood over him, blocking the
sun.
A man in his middle years, powerful, with a sullen
brow.
The man leaned closer and stared into his face.

The blue eyes searched, though what they were seeking
he could not guess.
He looked away, but the man hissed at him,
demanding his eyes.
He felt as a trapped creature must, when the hunter
appears and looks down at it.
He was ready to lunge with his hands, when the man
turned away and the sunset glared into his eyes.

There were hands at his shoulders, making him stand.

Behind him a building rose, taller than all of the others, with great doors and windows.
It filled up that side of the clearing.

They led him around it, and then through a place where the houses were lower and stood close to each other.
It was twilight here, but carts piled high with possessions were moving still, all in the same direction, away from the clearing.
People stepped back and stared as the men led him through. A young girl looked out from a doorway and met his eyes.
Her wondering face stayed with him as they passed through the crowd.

They turned where two houses leaned into each other, through a pass so narrow that the walls brushed his shoulders.
They came out in a shadowy clearing. No doors or windows looked in from the houses around it.
There was a small, round house there, shaped like the hives that hung in the birch grove.
A thick wooden bar held the door.

Inside there was food and drink on a low stool, and an oil lamp burning.
The walls were of wood, and the floor trodden earth.

As they closed the door, each man spoke to him.
Whatever the dove-words meant, they were not unkind.

He had trapped a fox once and not killed it, but brought it home to be tamed. He had spoken to it in that way. And the fox had escaped.

He sat on the bed of rushes beside the wall.
Overhead was a gap in the roof, too high and too small to climb through.
It was night up there, but the sound of the wagons and people went on, like thunder far off in the hills.

He took the lamp and made hand-shadows on the wall, as he did for his son some evenings before they slept.
He relieved himself near the door, and scraped at the earth till he'd covered it, like an animal.
The lamp was dying. The flame clung to life, fading and flaring till its last, tiny glow went out, though it lingered in his darkness a few heartbeats more.

He heard the wooden bar sliding back.
There was light again, another lamp in the doorway, and a woman holding it, closing the door behind her.
She came and knelt down in front of him.
The lamp threw her shadow up, over the walls and the roof.

She stared at him.
The smell of juniper smoke clung to her.
She reached out, fearful, and touched his cheek with her fingers.
He saw grief in her eyes.
She murmured something, as if to herself, then stood up quickly and went back to the door.

She left him in darkness.

Lying back on the rushes he could see two stars through the roof.
He watched them crossing that space, as he had watched stars moving so often before.
He pretended he might reach out and feel his wife's thigh, that his child was sleeping across in the darkness.

The stars moved slowly. He was guessing which beast they belonged to, high overhead.
The Fox or the Swan.
They would pass out of sight as the sky turned, and others would come.
The soft wheel-thunder went on through the night, and he fell into sleep, almost comforted by the sound.

If there were dreams, they were lost in the silence he woke to.
He listened for anything, but there was nothing.
Just the thudding of his heart, and the rushes scattering when he stood.

Someone had unbarred the door while he slept.
His bow and quiver lay outside at the threshold.
He picked them up, wondering, and ran.

The only sounds were his feet on the earth, and his breathing.
He ran between houses, passing the doorway where the child had stood, and there was no one, anywhere.

He came out in the clearing and stopped.
There was nowhere to hide, and nothing to hide from.
Where the crowd had flowed past the houses, and the echoes had stormed, there was only silence.
He stepped forward, careful, as though he might startle the air.
In all that space the emptiness was huge.

There was a smear of blood on the stone where he had fallen.
The wolf's skin was draped across the bench where he had sat.
His three gold pebbles lay together between the grey shoulders.

He looked up at the great house behind him.
There were birds wheeling silently, high overhead.

Grass was springing already between the stones at his feet.

The Doorway

There was a woman who did not remember her dreams, but in those dreams a door stood ajar, and an animal whisked out of sight as she turned her head.

There was daylight behind the door sometimes, and the murmur of voices receding, and the sound of a broom sweeping leaves on a flagstone path.

She did not remember the dreams, but she guessed they were there, and sometimes she found herself staring out at the garden, with nothing at all on her mind, as if she might stay like that forever.

On summer nights the scent of the dusk-blooming flowers filled her bedroom, and in winter a window stayed open, for the garden's sleep was as real to her as her own.

Her children had left, one by one, and their father before them, and the garden was like a wise lover whose language she shared. There were rocks and stones brought from everywhere she had travelled, and the wild saplings she had planted for each of her children had grown into trees. Her small plot of earth was both forest and clearing.

She was busy, and happy, and loved, but when she came home and shut the front door behind her, the sound of the lock as it fell into place meant freedom to her.

She knelt under the hazel tree, among flowers whose first seeds she'd scattered when the garden was new. She was picking out weeds, humming an old song under her breath. Above her a thrush sat tight on its nest, staring down through the leaves. The earth was loose and warm. She leaned forward and rested her cheek against it, and closed her eyes.

There was a scamper of animal feet, and the *hush hush hush* of a broom sweeping leaves across stones. The door stood ajar in the garden's wall. It was open towards her, when in all of her dreams it had opened outwards.

She slipped through without a thought, and forgot it at once, looking down the long gallery before her.

Through the windows on one side an animal was playing on the grass. It was a fox, she knew, though it did not seem quite like a fox. It danced on the grass with its shadow, and chased its tail, and ran on out of sight.

At the end of the hall was a double door, open. She was walking towards it, and as she did so a heaviness tugged at her breasts. They were full, and leaking, as though her long-ago children were hungering for her again.

The two couples who waited at the doorway seemed in awe as she approached. They bowed their heads as they parted to let her through, and watched her with timid and hopeful eyes. They were humbly dressed, and their faces were tired and worn.

She looked in those faces for traces of herself for she knew that they were, beyond living memory, her forebears. But all she found in their eyes was a wish to be chosen. Their need and humility shamed her. Each couple wanted her for themselves, but whichever way she looked the gallery repeated itself.

She stood, and they waited like servants. She searched their faces again, for who they might really have been long ago, in their passionate lives, and a flicker of pride in one woman's eyes made the choice for her. The other couple stepped backwards and turned away. She saw them leave in their meek, uncomplaining distress and her breasts ached for them.

But outside the window an animal played on the grass, and a double door waited at the end of the hall.

She was walking towards it, with the couple silent behind her, when she stopped, in the instant of forgetting. She grasped at the memory, as if for a dream that was slipping away. The man and the woman were staring at her, and she closed her own eyes against their disillusion.

A plain wooden door stood ajar where the windows had been.

It was autumn outside, with leaves drifting down on a terrace above the grass. A broom was leaning against the parapet, and the fox creature played in the leaves.

It was not the first time she had stood here. A thin mist was drifting across the fields, and a voice was calling her name.

There was no need to answer. The voice was her own.

She went to the parapet, waiting for the memories to return, for the smells and the sounds to complete the landscape before her.

The stone was rough and thrilling under her hands, and she stood looking out, with the leaves all around her feet, as if she might stay like that forever.

The Castaway

When a young priest in an old town fell into the sin of despair, his penance was to go back into the world and seek out his faith.

He stood in his room for the last time, with his suitcase half packed, and wondered what he should do. "You are only a castaway now," he told himself. He thought he might go back to the farm where his brother still lived, but the priest in the mirror called that cowardice. "That isn't the world," he said. "The world is a city now."

So the castaway rode the bus for a night and a day, and took a room in a cheap hotel near the station.

For a week he trudged the sidewalks, and rode the streetcars, and sat in cafés, watching and listening. He felt invisible, and was grateful for that. The people bewildered him.

He lay in bed with the sounds of other lives in the building around him.

"I am lonely for God," he whispered, and when the priest in him answered, "Perhaps God is lonely for you," he hated the glibness, the smugness of that.

He wandered through galleries and museums, but found himself most at home in the botanical gardens, with their misted glass walls and exotic vines. He bought crime novels from a second-hand stall and lost himself in their society.

Each evening he went to a shabby bar down the street and sat for an hour in the back room sipping his beer. One night a little stumpy man came in and sat down on the other side of the room. Every time he looked up the man was watching him, smiling and nodding as if they shared in an unspoken joke.

When he got up in irritation and left, the priest in him chided, "He is only a simpleton — isn't this where charity should begin?"

The next night he found the man sitting in the corner he thought of as his own, smiling up at him when he came in. He sat at another table and opened his book, but the words were a blur on the page.

"There are great things to be found in books, they say." The little man's voice was like a bird's. He let out a warbling laugh, and jigged his stumpy legs under the table.

The castaway could not tell why the words galled him so. He would not look up. "This is childish," the priest in him said, but "No," he muttered, and got to his feet, "there is something too knowing about that smile."

As he walked up the street he heard someone following, but each time he turned round to look there was no one there.

He chose the hotel bar instead the next night, and sat undisturbed for an hour with his beer and his book. But when he went to the door, past the crowd of men at the bar, a head turned towards him and there was the moon face of the little stumpy man winking and smiling up at him as he passed.

"Perhaps you are right," the priest in him said. "There is something dangerous about that creature."

At daybreak he called the farm and asked if he could come home. "There's plenty of work for you," said his brother. "Something to show for what was spent on your education." It was not said unkindly.

Two nights later the castaway sat at the farmhouse table, eating the meal that his brother's wife had prepared. Soon after dark, he climbed the narrow stairs to the room where he'd slept as a child. He lay looking up at the window and found himself whispering the words of his innocence: *One to watch and one to pray/And two to bear my soul away*. The priest in him knew this was simple nostalgia, but for all that not worthless.

Through the wall he could hear them making love. He covered his ears, but she was a handsome woman with a generous mouth, several months pregnant, and the vision played out in his mind.

He could not meet her eye in the morning, and she understood. "We want you to stay," she told him. "Your brother works too hard on his own." She pointed across the field to the cottage where his grandmother had lived out her days. "That can be your home," she said, "but I hope you will eat with us." She touched his shoulder and he felt a rush of love for her kindness. "Don't worry," she smiled. "You'll be earning your keep, believe me."

The weeks that followed were like time turning back on itself. Each day it seemed he could manage heavier loads, and though his brother's old work clothes hung loose on his frame, he felt he was shedding a tired, dusty skin.

They were careful with him, not demanding too much, and as he grew stronger, he thought less and less — too weary each evening to do more than cross the field and fall deep into sleep. The old cattle dog took to following him; it slept by the cottage door.

They left for a weekend, and he was in charge. He looked out at the land, and imagined that it was his own. Next week they would start the first haying; at month's end the lambs would be sheared and shipped off to the sales. The seasons turned in his mind. When Spring came again, their child would be taking its first steps.

He finished the chores and went off with the old dog, along the concession road. He passed other farms, each a world of its own, and a loneliness overtook him. The old questions returned.

"You could stay here forever," the priest in him said, "but if you mean to serve God through the work of your hands, you should choose the monastic life." He walked on towards the river. "That's a very big *if*," he said. "I'm just feeling my way. Let it be."

He stood on the high bank, looking down at the water. An angler was fishing beside some willow trees, casting over and over downstream. His line formed loops and arabesques in the sunlight, floated for a moment on the surface, and then flashed back again. The castaway stood mesmerized by his skill and the flowing stream. He watched where the line kept falling and there, where the sunlight went down through the water, he saw a big trout, suspended above the gravel. The line flew across, and he saw the trout rise to the fly and held his breath, but the line was whipped away at that moment, and the man resumed casting. This happened not once but twice, and then again, and the mad fancy struck him that if the angler stepped out from the trees and looked up, it would be the little stumpy man.

He called the dog softly and went back the way he had come.

In a dream that night he stepped out from a barroom door and found three men beating someone who lay whimpering on the ground. The castaway rushed to his aid, but the men laughed in his face and went off down the alleyway singing. He dropped to his knees and saw the face of the little stumpy man, the round, child's eyes filled with tears and bewilderment.

He awoke, and lay shaken with grief. The cottage was still in thrall to the nightmare. The priest in him whispered *by Thy great mercy defend us from the perils and dangers of the night*, but the dread remained. He opened the door and stood dressing himself, looking out at the first pale light in the East. The dew was thick and cold on the grass as he walked to the farmhouse.

He climbed the stairs and lay down in his brother's room. He thought of their lovemaking, and the child who would be born in the Fall, perhaps in this bed, and he fell back to sleep. When he woke, the sun was high and he was far behind with the chores.

He ran out to feed the lambs and open their pen, and then worked till the late afternoon. By the time he went out with the dog to bring back the lambs, there were dense clouds in the west and the air was still, with a queer violet light everywhere. It grew dark too early, and when the wind came it swooped onto the farm, scouring the puddles in the yard and rattling the tin on the barn roof. He went down to the stable just as the downpour began. The trees were loud in the darkness, and the rain lashed his face.

But the stable felt all the more sheltered for the tumult outside. The milk cow had come in on her own and was waiting for him. He sat on the stanchion's edge and began to milk, breathing in the moist animal warmth, resting his cheek on her flank. The milk hissed into the pail, while all around the barn was the noise of a storm at sea.

The lights dimmed and flickered, grew bright for a moment and then left him in the darkness. Flashes of lightning picked out the yard and the house and lingered in his eyes. The cow shifted and grumbled, but he soothed her and kept the milk flowing. Through the open door he saw a light coming through the rain; a figure with a lantern appeared and stepped inside. The little stumpy man hung the lantern on a nail and his shadow climbed the wall, and then shrank back down as he knelt in the straw. His smile appeared under the cow's belly, as he set to work on the two far teats.

There was no denying the harmony of it, the steady pulse of the milk through their hands. The castaway thought of the times when his sister and he had milked together, racing through the chore to get free, to go out and play.

The milk foamed up in the pail. "I don't know who this is," the priest in him said, "but I think it may be the Devil." The castaway leaned into the cow's side and answered himself: "What use would the Devil have," he said out loud, "for a man who does not believe?"

The little man's laugh was a mad bird's filling the stable. His hands were so deft, though. In no time at all he was done with his share, and was stripping the teats of their last thin drops.

"Who are you?" the castaway asked. "Where do you come from?"

"Hereabouts, thereabouts," the little man said. "It's all the same, you know." He reached under and gripped the castaway's hands, so that two hands were milking each teat together. It was the strangest feeling.

Their eyes met over the milk pail. "Don't worry your head," chirped the stranger, and when the milking was done he took down the lantern and went out into the storm without looking back

The castaway stumbled through rain and darkness, up to the house. At some point in the night he woke to a stillness all around. He opened the window to the sound of trees dripping, and smelled the earth washed clean.

There was a dance in the village hall the next Saturday night. His brother's wife came to find him. "You have to come with us," she told him. "You must let people get to know you." She looked at him gravely. "We're allowed to have fun, you know." He dreaded the prospect, but he knew he should not refuse.

There were fiddles and guitars, and an out-of-tune, battered piano. People of all ages came and mingled; they all seemed to know each other, they made shyness feel like a sin. The castaway stood watching near the door, perplexed and ashamed, till his brother's wife beckoned him over. "Come on, sobersides," she said. "Just throw yourself into it." He saw how gracefully she moved, despite the child in her womb, and when a woman took his hand and turned him around, he felt something break from its moorings. The lilt of the fiddles crept into his heels, until he was laughing and moving without any thought of himself.

For a moment he thought he saw angels in all of those faces, caught up in the dance, and he closed his eyes in delight. When he opened them he was passing the band on the stage, and there was the little stumpy man, playing the fiddle, smiling his child smile, his eyebrows and heels keeping time with the tune. The castaway laughed out loud, and the fiddler got to his feet and played wildfire jenny.

The castaway danced through the night. He danced with women, he danced with children, he danced with his shadow outside on the lawn.

He looked up at the stars, and the priest in him held his peace.

Rendezvous

There was a man who came home from the war and did not find peace.

He walked through the town and saw faces with empty eyes. He saw deadly smiles.

He sat in the rainy park and saw children who screamed with happiness, running for cover.

His wife said that he cried out in his sleep, yet he held his dreams at bay. He lay half-awake beside her each night till the dawnlight seeped through the blinds. When he woke hours later, dry mouthed in the empty house, he could taste the desert, the sour, clogging dust that had crept into their tents and their clothing, and merged with their sweat.

He went to the town library and sat reading by the window, but nothing made sense to him now. Each page was forgotten as it turned. The people walking by were like words on a page.

There was a time before, and a time before that, and he was lost somewhere between them.

He had run away from his youth in the Old World, drifting through fifteen countries each stranger than the last, trusting to luck. He'd found work when he needed to, in love with inconstancy, till one night on a beach under southern stars he met a girl whose smiles called into question everything he pretended to know. They travelled together up the coast, and Time dogged their footsteps everywhere. He loved her so much that after she left her face floated before him upon the sky and the trees and the heartless expanse of the ocean.

He'd signed on as a deckhand with a cargo ship, believing that luck had given way to destiny, and followed her back to her home in the New World. When he wrote to his parents, his first contact in more than five years, he'd enclosed a photograph of his bride, and himself in uniform. His father had been a soldier in more dangerous times; a circle of sorts was closing.

Their dreams became plans and the map of their future was plain, but the dangerous times had returned. The peacetime army convulsed with the world around it, and was sent off to fight for a land that had scarcely known peace in a thousand years.

In that country whose borders were not its own, and whose legends were all of invasion and fratricide, there was no one to trust.

They were hostages there. The enemy's features were as obscure and shifting as the weather. The barren hills and the orchards below drank the blood of invader and villager with weary indifference. A knife was as deadly as a warplane.

When he came home, the ambushes followed him.

The face that floated before him now, against his wife's quiet breathing and her warmth beside him in their bed, belonged to a boy he had killed.

He had knelt by a broken wall, holding his enemy's hand as it twitched towards death. The dark eyes had glared into his. The orchard was in blossom, birds circled in the white sky, the hills looked down. And for all that he wished to offer, he knew that his touch was killing the boy a second time. The hatred froze; his reflection creased and evaporated on the sightless eyes.

There was nothing to share. His wife could not bear his aloneness.

She held the child who had been born in his absence like a shield between them.

"I cannot be mother to you both," she told him. "I look at you, and you turn into someone else. When you touch me, I feel myself changing too."

He watched her closing the gate, her father standing beside the car, the child at her shoulder.

That night two men followed him as he walked home from a bar. He turned and laughed at them. "If you come one step closer," he said, "I will kill you both." They stared at him. "Are you out of your mind?" one said, and the other called out, "Get a life," as they crossed the street.

His wife's scent lingered in the living room. He fell back on the couch, listening in the silence to the sound of his heart, and found himself haunted not by the desert or the dying insurgent's face, but by a time long before.

Half a world away, where people were going to work while he lay in darkness waiting for sleep to come, water swirled under an old stone bridge.

On the low cliff above was a ruined tower, and a wall.

Sleep yielded to memory, and the river that had run underground since his sixteenth year flowed out in the air again.

Upstream, out of sight round the river's bend, the mouth of a ravine. The trails through the woods.

He could hear and smell. It was the air of his innocence.

Two days later, looking down through the clouds at the coastline of the Old World, he saw that the circle would finally close.

He drove out of the city in a rented car, on a freeway that could have been anywhere, until he turned onto old country highways and then along hedge-bound lanes that had traced the land's contours long before cars were imagined. He crossed two bridges and passed the grey hillside school, with its high dormitory windows, where he'd spent those troubled years. It all felt like scenery, familiar yet unreal, until he parked on the cobbled square of the little market town. The street swayed like a ship's deck as he stood looking around. The ground floor shops had new faces, but the stone upper storeys remembered. A young ghost went before him down the narrow lane to the riverside and along by the old mill, converted now to a tea house, to the bridge at the town's end.

He leaned on the parapet, staring down at the brown water, the pale flanks of the riverbed just visible in the shallows, the clifftop ruin's reflection. He looked up at the tower. An infamous king had stared out from those battlements long ago, in a time of civil war. The bridge remembered, or perhaps did not. The stone was cold to his hands. Five hundred years, or ten, so much was unchanged — the water rushing against the piers below, the rock doves sallying from the tower, the riverborne scent of the dales.

Across the bridge, where the road began its climb towards the hills, he vaulted the low wall and went down, at a run, to the riverbank. He was shedding the years — when he next looked back, the bridge and the town had vanished; only the ragged tower could be glimpsed through the hanging woods.

This had been his escape and refuge, yet how little he'd noticed back then. The river itself, its surface ripped and distorted here by the stones of a washed-away ford, had been merely a background to his solitudes. Now each thorn bush and furrow on the narrowing field was edged and distinct. As he left the path he felt the same cramping below his ribs, the same coppery taint in his mouth that had come before every patrol.

He saw himself as if from a lifetime's distance: a tiny figure crossing the water meadow to vanish into the trees.

The river's voice recedes and dies out. The forest hushes everything, but the hush discloses echoes, bird calls, and then the chuckle of running water. When you come to the stream the little valley reveals itself, aslant through the hillside, a sanctuary.

The water tumbles, fast and clear, through miniature rapids and pools. It is full of voices, confiding, conspiring. You can kneel and fill your cupped hands, or lean out to drink straight from the surface, breaking your reflection, imagining yourself an outlaw, a tiger, a deer.

There are animal trails to choose from, branching off through the green, filtered light and then branching again, like veins in a spreading leaf; but one in particular leads up to the clearing where wild garlic grows and beyond it the great beech tree with roots so wide and exposed that you can hide between them. The prison house shades disperse. You close your eyes and open them to the rumour of surf in the treetops, where the swaying branches are seaweeds in a lagoon.

The woods are a cavern, too: the way a wood dove's crooning throbs in the stillness, and behind that a remote, measured thudding that might come from underground or from far up the valley, but is surely your own heartbeat, taken up by the forest, your blood whispering through like the stream.

You have never shared this place. Just once you came up through the woods, hand in hand with a girl from the town, and then shied away down another trail. You were sure that you loved her, but your instinct knew better.

You fondle the tree roots with unconscious love. You become what you see. A small butterfly, drab as a moth, is dallying close to the earth, by a sprawl of red fungus. A dead leaf hangs in a spider web. Something moves at the edge of your sight. A rabbit comes into the open with a slow, hunching gait, and stops just a few feet in front of you. It twitches its nose and scuffs at its ear with a hind foot. The round, lustrous eyes are oblivious – you are one with the tree roots you see mirrored there.

But you *are* being watched. You look up and as the rabbit bolts, scuttering out of sight, you see someone standing across the clearing.

You stare at the ground, not knowing what you should do. Your leg begins tremoring uncontrollably, as the man walks over and stands, looking down at you.

"You're here after all," he says, quietly, softly. "Now I don't know what to say." The voice is vaguely American, the way he said "after," and now, as if puzzled, "Where's your book? There was always a book."

You fumble at your jacket pocket, avoiding his eyes. The trembling betrays you. When you tug the book free, he squats down and reaches for it. His hand is like yours but much stronger, and weathered, with a plain gold ring on one finger.

You glance up, and stare. The world is looking at you sideways. The mouth is bitter, the cheeks so tight on the bones, but there's only fondness as he turns the book over. "I've read it so often, I ought to know it by heart." He holds it up to his face, and breathes in its smell. "I left it in a chai shop," he says, with a little shrug. "When I went back to get it, it was gone."

He opens the book to the title page, then back to the flyleaf where your signature is. Your eyes meet; the moment of sadness is unbearable. "Let me in," he says and turns to wedge himself, shoulder to shoulder, between the roots.

You hold the book on your knees, flipping from chapter to chapter with their wild illustrations. Your hands keep touching. You know what is happening; you want it; but there's fear mingled in with the wanting.

"Oh Jesus," he says, leaning back against the tree's smooth bark, "I only wish." He closes the book and his hand slips down and touches you as gently, and knowingly, as you've ever touched yourself. The trembling dissolves.

"Let's just be still," he says. "Let's imagine we're dreaming."

"Daydreaming," you think.

"I was always good at that!"

The double cry of a pheasant rings out somewhere. In these woods you can never tell what direction sounds come from. Your head falls against his shoulder; you breathe in the smell of his skin, the bare neck; you feel like a girl.

The closer you come, the stronger his arm draws you to him. You are breathing together; you hear a name called, not your own.

Then your heartbeat loud in the woods; the low scent of wild garlic; a weakness all through you.

Your eyes open. He is watching you, his features gaunt and uncertain. The book lies where it fell, lodged against the grey root. He gets to his feet.

"Don't follow me," he says, and walks quickly across the clearing.

He steps into the trees, looks back, and then vanishes down the trail. A minute later his voice calls out from below, like a faraway bird's.

"Don't follow me."

Gramarye

Honesty bloomed in the witch's garden, and thrift stitched its way through the stone path to her door.

She came with the snowdrops, and left with the swallows, but a woodpile of birch and wild apple was stacked by the gate and smoke rose from her chimney all summer long.

She sat reading by the hearth while the afternoon sunlight crept in across the room towards her chair. A yellow bird sang in its cage by the window, and her cat stared out through the glass at the willow tree that shielded the house from the lane.

There was a girl staring back through the leaves. She had come with her cousin on a dare, and now they were spies, looking over the wall and into the witch's home.

The cat yawned and the witch looked up from her book. Her lips were moving.

"Do you think she can see us?" the girl whispered. "It looks like she's talking to us."

"Or singing," said her cousin. "She's casting a spell on us!" And they cycled madly back to the village, laughing in make believe terror.

The girl's uncle cut wood for the witch, and raked her leaves in the fall. He kept an eye on her place in the winter months, too, and laughed at the stories. "There's nothing strange about her," he said. "She keeps to herself is all. No harm in that. She knows flowers better than anyone."

But "Oh," said the aunt, "you're in deep trouble now, my girl. She'll have hexed you for sure. One of these days you may find yourself growing a tail." And each time the girl walked by, her aunt would glance down, as if she were looking for signs of that sprouting tail. The girl's mother took it up too. It was all a great joke.

But the young people knew better.

There were the five who'd gone down to skate on the long pond and had stopped at the witch's house. They pelted it with snowballs, and broke a window, and within the hour felt the ice crack under them, just as the window had cracked. Two boys and a girl fell through, out of sight, and the merest miracle carried them all to the open patch of water above the weir.

The teenager who worked each Saturday in the general store told how she'd pulled a rude face at the witch's back, forgetting the mirror on the wall between the shelves. The witch had just smiled at her, but that night, as her boyfriend was driving her home from a party, a black dog ran out in front of them and they went off the road at the bend above the old quarry. The car had hung teetering on the edge of the cliff, and they sat there for hours, not daring to move, until someone drove by in the morning and sent for help.

And there was the teacher's son who fired two stones from his slingshot at the witch's cat, where it sunned itself on her steps. The witch had come out, and pointed her finger at him without a word, and on his way home the ambulance had sped by, taking his little sister to the hospital. She lay between life and death, at death's door they said, for almost a week before she awoke from her coma.

There were other stories too. It seemed to the girl that the witch was the most interesting thing about the backwater town.

They'd come down from the city to help look after her grandma. The old lady was dying, and worse than that, they said she was losing her mind. The stroke she had suffered at Christmas had stolen most of her words, and she passed the days now in her grey wing chair by the window. Sometimes, when the family was gathered and talking, her eyes became bright and watchful, even gleaming with laughter or mockery, but most of the time they stared out with intense concentration at nothing at all.

The girl was not afraid of the physical things, the nodding and throat clearing, the smells sometimes, the shawl-twitching fingers, the webs of drool to be wiped from the tremoring chin; it was the vanishing of her grandmother, the strong, humorous woman full of stories. They had always felt like conspirators, sharing a language that had skipped a whole generation. Now she could not bear to look into the faded brown eyes which all too often seemed to be gazing right through her.

Instead, she went off with her every day, pushing the wheelchair along the riverside path out of town. Walking behind, she could pretend that her grandma's eyes were alert as her own and she talked to her as though nothing had changed. But really, it was a way to be alone. At home she had taken for granted the hours she could spend with herself, but here in her aunt's house, and sharing her cousin's bedroom, there was always someone else.

Each day she walked further, turning off down the overgrown towpath that her cousin had showed her, guiding the wheelchair over ruts and between the young bushes. It was better than being alone, because thinking out loud made things clearer. She would be a teenager in just a few weeks and she had many opinions. She had questions, too, even secrets she'd kept from herself until now. The grandmother listened, and sometimes her answers came in the girl's own voice.

Across the fields you could see the big weeping willow where the cousins had spied. The thought of it cast a spell, and the witch found her way into their conversation.

"Did you know her, Grandma? You must have. Do you remember when she first arrived?"

They stopped by the ruined lock, above the dried up canal, with their backs to the town.

"How old would you say she is? And where does she go in the winter? Where did she come from? What brought her here in the first place?"

The questions hung in the air and as no one had told her, and she couldn't have guessed, that the witch's house had once belonged to her grandmother, the girl began a story of her own as they started back towards home.

"Well, suppose she was someone's dark secret and they gave her away to the Gypsies, or the Indians, or maybe she was left by the wayside and found, yes, and she grew up speaking the language of birds and trees and stones, and then one day when she was thirteen they gave her her mother's ring and a purse with some gold coins, or a locket with a lock of hair — no, she found them hidden in a doeskin pouch behind the stairs and it wasn't a lock of hair, of course, it was a picture of her young mother, no, no — actually I bet the picture was of a house by a path through the woods they'd passed once in their wanderings, so she ventures forth, and gets lost, naturally, but with help from an owl that she rescues from a snare she comes out in a clearing, and there is the house from the picture, and she goes and knocks on the door, and — "

The wheelchair lurched against a stone, and her grandma cried out, "Ha!" as though she had been jolted out of sleep.

"Are you alright, Grandma?"

But her grandmother's eyes were smiling at her, and the pale lips trembled in an effort to speak.

The girl leaned closer, their faces almost touching, and she heard the faint words, *"Always listening."*

"Oh I *knew* you were, Grandma," she said, though she hadn't truly believed until now that it might be so.

The old eyes called her back. She leaned closer again. *"Finish story,"* she heard.

She kissed the smooth forehead. "I'll try," she said, and tucked in the rug around the child-like legs before she set off again.

"Well, for half the year she has to go back into the wilderness or she'll lose, or maybe she already can't understand the wild things and the stones anymore, their language is fading, no, no because you see her father was really a Gypsy, or an Indian, and so . . . and so . . ."

Make believe had always been part of their language. Her grandma was known for her brisk, no-nonsense views, her impatience with sentimentality, yet she treated some imaginary things as quite matters of fact. There were guardian angels, and spirits of hedgerows and fords, and she paid close attention to her dreams, the Wednesday night ones in particular.

There was a bookcase in her house, on the landing, that was reserved for what she called *Gramarye*. For a long time the girl thought she was saying *Grandma read.* It was in fairy tales that their love for each other had begun.

"But suppose, Grandma, that the father was an Elfin Knight, or perhaps he was the *grandfather,* and the witch is the child of the lost girl instead – oh . . . "

Her birthday gift each year since she was born had been a book of stories. There were twelve of them, each named for a colour and some of them faded and worn, and each year the gap in the *Gramarye* bookcase had grown wider. The banknotes tucked into the books had changed colour too since the year she turned seven, from brown to blue to purple to green, more generous each time.

The *Lilac Fairy Book* had come last year, and her grandma had written on the fly leaf, in her blue-black ink: *This is the last one. You will be a young woman soon, but don't forget.* The crisp enclosed bill had been rose-red, with a fierce snowy owl staring out from the frozen tundra. It was more money than she had ever held in her life.

Above Grandma's inscription were her own grandmother's words, and in two of the books, the *Blue* and the *Red,* there were faded birthday blessings from two even earlier grandmas. It seemed to the girl that these gifts reached back almost forever.

The witch belonged, irresistibly, to the world of those books. She was hardly ever in town, the store owner delivered her groceries, and she never had visitors. The girl had caught that glimpse of her through the leaves, but each night, when they'd turned off their bedside lamps, the willow tree across the fields, and the cat in the big bay window, stole into her thoughts, maybe into her dreams.

"She has a cat and a bird, and all manner of flowers in her garden, and a fire in midsummer. I think I shall go and visit her. Do you think I should, Grandma? She has no friends, though perhaps she doesn't want any of course. But if I mean her no harm, and tell no one I've been there, what harm could she wish me? Do you think I should go?"

As the wheelchair trundled across the iron bridge into town, she took the old lady's nodding as total agreement.

She went off on her bicycle the next afternoon, the way that her cousin had showed her. "You've got such a nerve," she told herself, as others had told her before, but when she turned up the lane and the willow came closer, she began to lose heart. "I'll see if she's out in her garden," she said. "That will be a sign. If she isn't there, I'll forget it."

But the witch was there. She was kneeling at a flower bed, close to the gate, in a floppy green hat and gardening gloves. She looked younger than the girl had expected.

"And what can I do for you?"

The eyes were hazel, watchful but amused. It was a kind face, apart from the scarred, twisted lips.

"I don't believe in witches."

The witch sat back on her heels. "No, I don't suppose you do," she said. "What *do* you believe in?"

The girl felt herself flushing to the roots of her hair. "I'm sorry," she said. "That was rude of me wasn't it?"

"Not rude," said the witch, and she started to pull off her gloves, "but very direct. And you haven't answered my question." Her voice was low, and gentler than her words.

"I don't think I know how to," the girl said. "I'm sorry."

"Two *I'm sorries* are quite enough for one afternoon," the witch said, and got to her feet. Her loose smock had open pockets across the front; it was the same faded green as her hat. "You'd better come in for tea, and think about it."

"All right," the girl said.

The witch's crooked smile woke a host of fine lines around her eyes. It was impossible to guess how old she might be. "You don't stay abashed for long, do you?" she said. And she came and unlatched the gate. She was a slight woman, not much taller than the girl, and though her hair was streaked with a silvery grey, it was tied back in what was almost a ponytail,

The girl followed her up the path where low pink flowers bristled between the flagstones.

The witch turned, with her hand on the doorknob.

"What's your name?"

"Melissande."

"No it isn't."

"Well, it will be one day, when I can choose."

"Fair enough," said the witch. "There's no need for names here anyway." She held the door open, and the girl stepped into a kitchen where strings of onions and garlic hung by a window, and the air smelled of herbs and lemons.

"Oh wow," she whispered. She spun around on the blue-tiled floor, taking in the pinewood dressers, the copper pans hanging above the stove, the calm, uncluttered space around the plain, heavy table.

Through the next door the living room was full of light. There were gay rugs like islands on the pale wooden floor.

"It's so much bigger and brighter than it looks from outside," the girl said. "You must love it."

The witch put her hat and gloves on the bare wooden table, and filled a kettle at the sink.

"Go and look around," she said. "I'll come through with the tea when it's ready."

The girl slipped out of her sneakers and stepped barefoot into the room. The bay window was like a room of its own, with big cushions on the floor beneath it. The cat sat on the window seat with its back to her, looking out. And there was another window, to her right, and beside that a black writing desk with elegant legs, and a painting above it of an old house among windswept trees, with low rocks in the foreground.

Across the room a staircase went up, forming a partial wall beside the fireplace. This was the space that felt the most lived in. The hearth was of grey flagstones, like those on the path outside, and a big rocking chair faced the fire, with a table beside it, a lamp and a pile of books.

It was strange how fire drew you, even on a hot July day. The girl went to it, spreading her hands as if to warm them. Two logs burned lazily on an iron cradle, and there were more logs in a basket, waiting. On the other side of the fireplace was a rush-seated stool and – oh, a real witch's broom.

She took the broom and sat on the stool, with the rough twigs between her feet, and leaned her cheek against her hands where they held the broomstick.

A fire was like water under a bridge – you could stare for hours, and almost not have to think.

She leapt up. The witch was standing at the kitchen door, with a cup in each hand, watching her.

The girl held out the broom. "Is this your midnight steed?"

For a second, the witch's eyes were like stones. Then she laughed. It was a young laugh, girlish and full of amusement. "Oh yes," she said. "Over the rooftops and under the stars, peering in windows, pilfering dreams."

The girl's cheeks were burning. "That was bold of me, wasn't it?"

The witch laughed again. "Bold? That must be your mother's word for you." She held out one of the cups. "Here, try this if you dare."

She had taken off her smock. Her skin was pale below her neck, and a green stone hung there on an almost-invisible chain.

The cup was white and delicate; the girl could see the tea's shadow through it. The steam smelled musky, but the first sip was like rainwater might taste if you drank it out of a lily.

"What kind of tea *is* this?"

"It's *kvann* that you're smelling – *angelica*."

"Will it turn me into a toad?"

The witch looked at her sideways: "More likely a barn owl, don't you think?"

The girl's eyes widened. The barn owl was her special bird. She had a poster of it at home, over her bed, staring with its white heart-face from a castle window.

She went and leaned the broom against the chimney breast. On the mantel, at eye level, was a cluster of treasures just like her altar of 'foundlings', as her mother called them, on the bedroom dresser at home. A banded snail shell, an ivory ring, curious stones and weathered pieces of wood. A bird's skull, a red and grey feather, a speckled sea shell with a flesh-pink cavity. And one stone that seemed to have raised white flowers all over it. She sipped the sweet tea and reached out with her left hand.

"No, don't touch, please. Just look."

"I wouldn't hurt anything."

"Some things don't want to be touched – the things from the wild – my hands are the only ones that have held them."

"What can I touch, then? You didn't mind the broom."

"Anything that's made to be used – the furniture, crockery, the books. *Things men have made and breathed soft life into.* A good angel wrote that."

"I can't tell when you're serious," the girl said. "Do you believe in angels then?"

"They are never far away. You might be an angel, sometimes, you know; an angel might inhabit you for a while, without you knowing it."

"But you said a good angel."

"Ah yes," the witch sighed. "I'm afraid there are bad ones too."

The girl felt suddenly awkward.

"Can I sit in the rocking chair?"

"Certainly you may."

The girl flung herself into the big chair, and kicked with her heels. The witch pulled the stool out, a little way onto the hearth, and sat with her knees drawn up, watching. She held her cup in both hands, and when she drank, and her lips disappeared, she looked quite different. In that light her face was unlined.

For a while there was no sound but the creak of the chair and the muttering fire.

The girl stopped, and took a book from the table beside her. "*Piano Quintet in A Major,*" she read. It was a musical score. She felt her usual shame about the piano lessons.

"What do you play, what instrument?"

"I have a harpsichord in my winter house. Here, I just read."

"You read the music?"

"Yes, these are my summer books."

"And you can hear it?"

"Don't you hear when you read?"

"I suppose," the girl said. "But look, you have to read five or six lines at a time. I couldn't do that."

"But you do," the witch said. Indoors, her eyes were more green than hazel. They seemed to grow as she talked. "We read sentences and paragraphs, not words. And you're seeing things as well as hearing them, aren't you? And feeling too, and often remembering and imagining, all at the same time."

"I'll have to think about that," the girl said, and looked around for something else. She pushed herself up from the chair. "Where did your bird go?"

"My bird?"

"The yellow bird in the cage by the window."

The witch's eyes looked into her. "I think you must have dreamed that," she said. *"A robin redbreast in a cage Puts all heaven in a rage."*

"Oh," said the girl. "And I thought that your cat would be black too."

"Ah no," said the witch, "he has to be grey." And she creased up her eyes and crooked her fingers and cried in a thin, cackly voice, *"I come, Greymalkin!"*

As if it had heard, the cat looked towards them and opened its mouth in a huge, slow yawn.

"Or perhaps you haven't read that yet," the witch said in her normal voice.

"You're like my grandma used to be — full of poems and sayings."

"That's what memory's for, is it not?"

The girl frowned. That didn't make sense to her. She was about to ask the cat's name, when her eye was caught by the painting across the room.

She heard the witch laugh behind her.

"What's so funny?"

"You're such a honey-bee, darting from flower to flower."

"My auntie calls me a flibbertigibbet."

"That's a word with a history," the witch said. "But no, I think honeybee suits you much better."

"Anyway," said the girl, "will you tell me about this picture? Is it a real place?"

The witch set down her cup. "It's as real as you and me."

"I love stone houses. It looks very old."

"It's old and it's new. A dead friend built it for me from the stones of a derelict lighthouse."

"Have you many dead friends?"

The witch's eyes did not leave the painting. "Oh yes," she said softly. "Have you?"

"Just my dad. And soon my grandma I suppose."

She moved back a step. "Where I'm standing, would I be on the seashore?"

"Not quite, no. You're by the grey boulder where I love to sit." The witch came and stood beside her. "The sea pinks grow here and all along the clifftops. Behind us there's a goat path going down to the cove."

"Are there goats?"

"They like to browse on the seaweed. And out in the cove there's a flat rock, you can almost walk to it at low tide, and sometimes the seals come and bask there in the sun."

"Seals."

"You can hear them on calm nights, slapping their tails and calling."

"Mermaids," the girl whispered.

"I like to think so."

There was a thud on the floor behind them. The cat was strolling towards the staircase, its tail erect and curled at the tip.

"When I look out from my workroom window," the witch said, "I can see across the straits to the islands. And downstairs I have a painting of *this* house, so I won't forget."

"I've never been to the sea," the girl said. "Except when I was a baby, too young to remember."

"You'll grow accustomed to it. And you'll miss it when you're away. It calls to you in your dreams. You'll wake up wondering why everything is so quiet."

The girl had never met anyone who looked you so much in the eyes.

There was another thud. The cat had leaped up three stairs and was stretched out there, flexing his paws with another great yawn. The girl went over.

"Will he let me pet him?"

"Let him come in his own good time."

There was a window on the landing where the staircase turned back on itself. A tree was pressing its leaves against the glass.

"What's up there?"

"Up there is upstairs."

The girl set her foot on the first stair. "Am I allowed to look?"

"Yes, if you wish." The witch came and leaned on the bannister. In a mock whisper she said:

> *But as she passed, they cried "Beware*
> *The wicked turning of the stair."*

"I don't know that story," the girl said.

"Perhaps it's waiting for you to write it."

Their faces were close enough that the girl could smell lavender. The witch's eyes were as young and clear as her own. She might have been beautiful once, if it weren't for those poor lips.

"How old are you?"

"What did your grandmother say, the first time you asked her that?"

"As old as my tongue and a wee bit older than my teeth."

"And there's no better answer."

"But how do you know that I asked her?"

"Well, what child doesn't?"

"I *would* like to write books someday," the girl confided.

"I expect you will, too. But are you going to find out the rest of the story or not?"

"Yes I am," said the girl, *"Beware, beware!"* and ran laughing, past the cat, up to the landing.

There were little pears among the leaves at the window, green and brown, almost within reach. There was a low table, too, with another altar of treasures, and against the wall beside her –

"What's this?"

The witch climbed two steps towards her. "Ah, that."

It was like a cloak on a shop window mannequin, but flat, with a spindle of dark wood where the head would have been. The fabric was velvet, dark green, and silvery where the daylight caught its folds. Perhaps it was a curtain. It was fastened below the spindle with a braided red cord.

"Is it a secret?"

The witch untied her hair and shook it loose so that it lay across her shoulders. "The best secrets are the ones people wouldn't believe even if you told them."

"So can I look then?"

The witch came a step closer. "If you must and you will, then you shall and you may."

The cord felt like silk. When the girl tugged, the cloak fell open at once.

There was an oval mirror, as tall as herself. A woman in a blue dress was looking back at her.

For a moment she thought it was her aunt Nora, her father's sister, but no, she was different. The face was familiar, though, the expression –

"It's me, isn't it?"

The witch came up and sat at the edge of the landing. "It's who you *will* be."

The girl stared. The grown-up her seemed unaware, as if she was simply watching herself in her own mirror. She did not move when the girl did.

Something rubbed against her leg, and there was the cat, in the mirror too, arching its back by the woman's foot. In the room behind them she could see the edge of a table or desk, and a window beyond, with blue sky, like the sky through the pear tree's leaves, and a curtain shifting in a breeze.

"She looks happy," the girl said.

"And that's a blessing for you."

"So it tells you the future?"

The witch got to her feet. "*Then goes backwards and forwards*," she said, and she stepped behind the girl.

The woman in the blue dress had turned away and was going towards the window. The cat followed her.

And there in the mirror stood a child, perhaps seven or eight, with short blonde hair, dressed in striped dungarees. She was staring straight ahead, crossing her eyes and poking out her tongue, trying to touch her nose. The witch's cry of laughter set the girl laughing too.

"Is that really you?" she said.

"At my age, the glass looks backwards. It's good to be reminded."

Behind the child witch, the woman was indistinct now, gazing out through the window.

"But suppose," the girl said, "I was going to die when I was still young?"

The child leaned closer, and the witch's voice whispered in the girl's ear: "In that case, Sweetheart, I would never have let you come up."

She reached forward and drew the cloak closed again over the glass.

The girl looked into the witch's face. "And it never shows you just as you are?"

"You're a gem," the witch said. She took the girl's hand and drew her back to the stairs. "Yes, there are moments in your life – just one moment perhaps – when you are exactly who you are supposed to be. If you happened to look in the mirror then, that is who you would see."

The cat seemed to flow down before them. "What do you call him?" the girl asked.

"Sometimes Memory, sometimes Amnesia. Mostly, Cat."

"You're funny."

"Not scary?"

"Can't you tell?"

"Well that's good." She let go of the girl's hand. "And now it's time for you to leave and for me to get those irises back in the earth before they dry out."

"But," said the girl, "your young self in the mirror didn't have — "

"My mouth?" A shadow passed between them. "Yes, there was an accident. But I've always believed," she said as they walked towards the kitchen, "that when bad things happen it's really the angels sparing us from something much worse."

"I think you're brilliant," the girl said.

"Brilliant *and* funny. I wonder where you picked up that silver tongue."

The witch took her smock from the table and pulled it over her head.

The girl stepped back into her sneakers. "Thanks," she said. "Thanks for trusting me."

The witch smiled as she pulled on her gardening gloves. "Believe me, Dearheart, most people would just see a mirror."

"But I'd never tell anyone, ever."

The witch gave a little nod.

As they went down the path, she stooped and broke off a pink flower. "Here," she said. "A gift to you from the sea. From the cliffs above the cove." In the sunlight her eyes were hazel again. "And there I have planted honesty with seeds from this garden."

"That's a flower too?"

The witch went over by the apple tree and came back with a small, papery disk. There were flat round seeds inside it. "Fairy silver," she said. "You hide this in a corner of your garden, and see what will happen."

As the girl cycled off, she called back: "You'll see me again, you know," and imagined the witch's reply.

She pedalled back up the lane, laughing into the wind. She rode with no hands, and sang and wove till she reached the main road.

This was what glee meant.

She coasted past the towpath entrance and over the bridge. She was singing the song that she and her cousin had danced to the night before.

She was the luckiest girl alive.

The adults were wonderfully incurious about her comings and goings. They had other things on their minds, and were grateful for the time she spent with the old lady. So was her cousin. "You're great with old Nana," she said. "I find her creepy, though I know I shouldn't."

The girls had known each other all their lives. They listened to music together, and compared their breasts in the bedroom mirror, but the cousin had her own friends in town, and wanted to be with them, though the girl was not unwelcome. They would hang around the old store porch, or go off down the riverbank to the swimming hole under the white cliff.

One day as she lingered on the bridge, watching the swallows race their reflections on the water, a boy took her hand, and asked her to walk with him up to the Folly on the ridge. "I don't think I'm ready for that," she told him. "You're weird," he said, but no one was watching and he didn't seem too put out. In her mind she told him, "And you're not ready for that either, if you only knew," and looked in his eyes and saw that he did know that, actually. They smiled at each other and ran to catch up with the rest.

The next morning she had to struggle to come awake. Her cousin was dressed already, toying with her hair in the mirror. "You talk in your sleep, you know," she said.

The girl sat up in bed. "What about?"

"It's like hearing someone on the phone, like one half of a conversation.."

"And what do I say?"

"Well I'm not taking notes. I'm trying to get back to sleep."

The girl reached for her clothes. "Did I talk last night.?"

"Something about *But they'll miss me* and then *But will you always be there?* She looked up in the mirror: "So, is there *someone* I don't know about?"

"Don't be a cretin. Was that all?"

"The last thing was you sat up and said *Amnesia Cat* and laughed out loud." Her cousin left the mirror and bent to put on her shoes. "I was going to throw something at you, but then you shut up, thank god."

"I wonder if someone was having the other half of my dream," the girl said.

"You're truly weird ," said her cousin, and reached to pinch the girl's ribs on her way to the door.

The girl ran after her. "Bitch, perv, anarchist!" she yelled, and then shrieked and ran back into the bedroom.

She rolled on the bed in hilarious shame. Her uncle had been standing at the foot of the stairs, looking up, open-mouthed.

He wasn't there at the table when the girl came down, but each time their eyes met, the cousins broke out into helpless giggles. The women looked at each other. Her mother shook her head. "I suppose we were just as bad, heaven help us," she said.

Though the girl had forgotten her dreams, she remembered what she had decided as she'd waited for sleep.

But her grandma had had a bad night, they said. She had better stay at home. After lunch, though, they relented. "Just don't go too far," the girl's mother told her. "We have to be careful."

"I know," the girl said, but her mind was already on its way.

"It's a secret, Grandma," she said as she closed the gate. "I have a new friend, and you're going to meet her now." Her grandma did look very pale but her eyes were alive, and her head moved a little from side to side as if she was watching everything.

As they passed the towpath and headed instead up the hill, the girl said, "I wonder if you can guess." And bent to hear the old lady whisper, *"Caution."*

She laughed — it didn't mean *Be careful,* it was one of her grandma's quaint sayings. *You are a caution!* always said with a smile for her granddaughter's headstrong ways.

The hill seemed much longer today, walking and pushing, and the midsummer sun threw almost no shadow at all. By the time they turned into the lane the girl was too weary to talk. She leaned heavily on the wheelchair and went at a snail's pace.

She'd feel quite the fool if the witch wasn't home. But the witch was, of course. She came out at the back door as the gate clicked shut, and waited on the path.

"Hello Helen," she said. "It's good to see you again." And she took a frail hand from the old lady's lap, and held it in both of hers.

"How did you know Grandma's name?"

The witch looked up, puzzled. "But your grandmother grew up in this house. I bought it from her."

"How very strange," the girl said, "that no one ever said so."

"Well, it will be happy to see her again."

The grandmother was gazing up at the witch and struggling to speak. The girl leaned forward, straining to hear her.

"She said *dear Jessica*!"

"Ah," said the witch. "Then my secret's out."

She looked very slender beside the wheelchair, almost fragile in her long, dark dress. Her hair was loose, but swept to one side by a plain silver clasp. There was an amber bracelet on her left wrist.

"You're so elegant today," the girl said. "Did you know we were coming?"

She half expected the witch to say, "Well of course."

"On a day hot as this, I felt like staying indoors and reading."

"Tchaikovsky?"

The witch tossed back her hair, with that girlish laugh. "Something less earnest than that," she said. "Let's get your grandmother out of the sun."

Between them they eased the wheelchair over the threshold. The girl pushed it through to the living room, and reached down to loosen the security strap.

"Well?" said the witch.

"I suppose you can guess why I've come."

"Did you need a reason?"

All at once the girl found herself tongue-tied. She felt tired and foolish, and she wished she could just disappear. She was saved by the cat. It came flowing down the stairs and padded across the room, straight to the wheelchair. It sniffed at the rug around the grandmother's legs and leapt up onto her lap. The old lady gave a start, and then relaxed. The cat curled itself under the pallid hands, and closed its eyes.

"Wow," the girl said.

"Wonders will never cease," said the witch.

The girl took a breath. "You see," she said, "I thought that perhaps we could show my grandma the mirror."

She looked down. The silence went on forever.

"You are an extraordinary child."

"Only I didn't know if it had to be up there at *the turning of the stair.* Because we couldn't — "

"The mountain will come to Mohammed," the witch said. "Why don't you move the wheelchair to face the fire? "

She climbed to the landing and then came slowly back down. One hand was behind the mirror, holding it upright beside her, in its green cloak. They were like two people descending the staircase together.

She set it down on the hearth, and the girl manoeuvered the wheelchair in front of it.

"Go ahead, then."

The girl tugged the red cord, and watched her grandmother's face. The old eyes, almost closed now under their blue-veined lids, were suddenly wide open and a child's voice cried, "I remember!

"Yes, I remember. It was my birthday, and they let me stay up long past my bedtime." The old lips were mouthing the words, but it was the child in the mirror, a little girl in a brown dress with a wide lace collar, who was speaking.

Behind her was a room with a high ceiling, and a long table under a chandelier, laid out as if for a dinner party. The cat was not in the mirror, and there were no other people except the young witch – though not so young as before – and the grown-up girl – who had grey hair now, and a cane – and they were fading already, transparent phantoms in the grandmother's world.

The mirror had different rules.

"They gave me posset," the mirror child said. "They brought me posset, and they all drank my health."

She laughed and turned round to look back, and the witch said, "Well, we shall make her posset then. Come into the kitchen and help me – she's happy with her own company."

But the girl could not move. There were figures moving behind the child now – women and men in long-ago clothes who glided, as if they were dancing. She could not stop looking, but she wanted to, badly. She was getting scared, scared even of the mirror child who was once her grandma. It was as though her real grandma had vanished, for the girl could not drag her eyes from the mirror. She felt as though she was fading away herself. Where was she? Perhaps she would never come back.

She felt a gentle pinch at her cheek. The witch was standing there, with a small saucepan in her hand. The grandmother was gazing into the mirror world, eyes wide, her lips moving as the child chattered on. "Come now," the witch said. "I need you to help me."

The girl followed into the kitchen. "I was frightened to death," she said.

"So I saw, "said the witch. "That's the way with a venturing heart. Now, this is the first stage."

She was pouring thick cream into the saucepan.

The girl recovered herself. "So what is this 'posset'?"

"Just watch. The wine comes next."

It was a dusty bottle, with a galleon on the label. "Madiera," the witch said, "from the Islands of the Blest."

"Are you making a potion?"

"I suppose I am."

Then, "Can you hear that?"

The witch listened. "Yes, just," she said. "It's a very strong memory."

Beneath the child's prattle there were faint voices, as though a whole gathering of people were there. And music, even fainter, like a music box playing in a faraway room.

The girl let out a big sigh. "You couldn't make this up," she said. "No one would believe you."

The witch was stirring wine into the simmering cream. "Remember what I said to you, about secrets? Now will you warm this up with hot water, please?"

It was like a child's teapot, but with handles at both sides.

"What's this?"

"That is an old posset cup. Just fill it with hot water and rinse it out."

"You have everything, don't you?" the girl said.

"Well, actually, that came with this house. It was in the back of a cupboard. Now, bring it over and watch."

The witch set the cup down on the table and slowly poured in the potion. The girl watched the thick cream float up, and then a froth that rose through it slowly, almost to the cup's brim.

"There," said the witch. "I'll carry it through. Here's a cloth for her lap, and a napkin.

It's party time!"

The voices were gone as they walked through, but the mirror child was still talking " — because they said that when I was nine I might have a pony. Mother said that was much too young, but she was only teasing, and then we all laughed."

"Shoo, Cat," the witch said, and the cat leaped down with a chirruping cry. The girl laid the cloth across her grandmother's lap, and "Here you are Helen," the witch said, and "My posset," the child's voice cried.

"We'll set it down on your lap, now," the witch told her. And to the girl: "Take the spoon." It was china too, with the same swirled pattern as the cup. The old hands shook as they curled around the cup, though the hands in the mirror were steady.

"Now first," said the birthday girl, "you start with the grace." You could tell she was parroting an adult. "The grace is the foam on the top, and you mustn't eat greedily, and *never* wipe your mouth with your hand. That is what the napkin is for."

What a prim little creature she was, with her shoulder-length ringlets.

The girl wiped her grandmother's lips after every spoonful. The child in the mirror wiped her own. The witch stepped back, and stood watching by the fire.

"And then comes the custard. Remember, just a little at a time, be ladylike."

A sly look came into the grandmother's eyes.

"Then they let me take a sip from the spout, the real wine. I had such a good sleep that night."

The grandmother tilted her face towards the cup. The girl helped lift it to her lips, and when she had sipped, and a little had spilled down her chin, she let go, and sighed. Her hands lay open on her lap.

"This has been the best day of my life," the little voice said, and then the old eyes drooped, and Grandma's head fell forward into sleep.

The witch was standing by the mirror. She drew the cloak over it. "There," she said.

The girl reached for the cloth and the spoon, and stumbled against the wheelchair. The cup flew out of her hand, and smashed on the floor. Wine ran out in all directions.

She let out an anguished cry. "I'm so sorry," she sobbed. She was appalled and fearful.

The witch came and held both her shoulders. The green eyes looked into her, piercing and kind. "Nothing happens by accident," she said. "Don't worry about it. I'll clean up later."

"And oh," cried the girl, "It must be so late. They'll be wondering."

The witch helped her out through the kitchen, and came to the gate. "Goodbye, Helen," she said. "Sweet dreams, you old dear."

The girl ran back towards town, as fast as she dared, and her grandma slept on, despite all the joltings and turns.

Her uncle met them at the bridge. "They won't be too pleased," he said. "We've been looking all over."

"Oh stop fussing," the grandmother said, quite loud and distinct.

"Imagine that," said the uncle, staring down at her. "And look at you, Mother – you've got roses in your cheeks."

The girl's aunt was standing at the garden gate, her hands on her hips. She hurried forward, without looking at the girl.

"You all right, Mom?"

The old lady stared at her blankly.

"Well, no harm's done, I suppose," the aunt said. "She looks quite comfortable – though she'll need cleaning up."

Nothing more was said. That evening the girls went to a movie in the school gym. It was full of screams and murders and terrified babysitters hiding in closets. The audience was loud, and entirely young.

They walked home through the twilight.

"Can you keep a secret?" her cousin said.

"Of course I can."

"I had my first real kiss today. My whole body's on fire."

"Oh yuck," said the girl. "Who was it, that boy from the drugstore?"

"As if. You will never know."

"Then why did you tell me?"

"To drive you insane with envy."

They chased each other home under the streetlights.

The last thing her cousin said as she turned off her lamp was, "Try not to talk tonight, okay? I'd like to enjoy my own dreams, pretty please."

The girl lay awake for a long time, dispelling the stupid terrors of the movie before she could take herself back through the whole afternoon. What a secret they had, just herself and the witch and her grandma, and no one to disbelieve.

But some time in the small hours of that night the grandmother's heart stopped beating and the girl walked back in a dream where the pink flowers shivered in the wind and gulls hung beside her, wings motionless over the cove.

She stopped at the house door and looked out across to the islands. The sea wind was on her face, and a curtain billowed out from the window upstairs where a story lay waiting, unfinished, on her father's desk.

Why was everything so quiet all at once? She lay alone in the darkness.

She could hear her cousin's soft breathing across the room, and then the thin shriek of a barn owl, hunting somewhere out in the night.

She opened her eyes, and shut them again at once. The streetlight's glow through the curtains was breaking the spell. Her dream was fading out of reach.

The owl cried again, far away, and she pulled the sheet over her face. She closed her eyes tightly, shutting out every distraction and yes, there it was, the slow murmur of waves, the gulls crying. She could smell the sea, and see the islands, and the house was there as before.

And now she would open the door and go in, up the stairs, to the room with the desk and the mirror, and find out perhaps how the story will really end.

The Likeness

There was a man whose fame as a painter had come and gone.

He'd known bitterness, and envy, and doubt; but they too had passed.

He made a bonfire of what remained — all the drawings, the line and wash studies, that felt closer now to his heart than any signed canvas he had offered to the world.

He came and went through the afternoon, carrying the sheaves of paper out through his garden. Each shelf and drawer in his studio held an episode from a life gone by, but the dense rag paper was slow to burn and as the afternoon wore on, that life seemed less and less to have been his own. He was more involved in keeping the fire alive and trying to rid himself of the Italian overture that some word association had conjured up out of nowhere. The jaunty refrain played over and over in his head; he found his breath taking on its cadences; it refused to let go.

It was playing still when the garden lay in near darkness, and he stood with the last of his work at the studio window. The firepit glowed and winked, and a chill of unease eddied through his breast.

The frayed portfolio in his hands had lain in the studio closet since they'd bought the house, twenty years before. Even then it had been a relic of an earlier, innocent time.

He could hear his heart beating, as though it were somewhere outside him. The music had stopped, but then – when he took himself out of the room and down the back stairway to the garden – he was whistling it tunelessly under his breath again.

The portfolio was smaller than he remembered, but heavier too. He had taken it with him when he dropped out of art school, and it had gone with him everywhere, his second piece of luggage, through the years of love and poverty.

The garden smelled more like October than March now. There were lights on in the houses across the lane, and the neighbours' pear tree by the fence was half silhouette, half underlit by the fire.

He held the portfolio at his hip, loosening the ties, and saw in the fire's light the stain like a hand splayed out across its surface.

Her foot had sent the bottle skidding as they danced in that spartan loft, whirling each other around, delirious. His first sale, his first commission, the offer of a show, all on that one rain-shrouded day. How they'd dropped to the floor and lain laughing there, licking the spilled wine, their cheeks pressed to the portfolio's skin, inching towards each other, kissing . . .

In the instant that he smelled the wine, the near-touch of her lips, the portfolio fell open and everything within spilled out into the pit. For a moment the fire was obliterated; then a line of flame ran around the pit, and the heap of drawings was all at once ablaze. The sheets of cheap, lightweight paper peeled away as they burned, with scorched, fleeting images as if from invisible ink. His young wife's back, her body turning in a doorway, her sleeping face, her hand at rest under lamplight.

He saw that he had done something wicked and must retrieve what he could.

He dropped to his knees, throwing the portfolio aside, and lunged with both hands, but the heat and pain made him rear back, and all he had done was scatter the unscathed drawings. Now the fire was winnowing them all; flakes of ash and charred paper were swirling around him in the glare; they seemed to bring the night closer.

He took breath, as though he were plunging into water, and forced his hand back through the flames, shielding his face with his other hand, groping blindly for what might be saved. His fingers closed and opened without any sensation but pain. His sleeve was on fire. As he scrambled away, a sheet of paper floated smouldering close to his face. He cried out and snatched it from the air, and then went stumbling back to the house where his shadow on the wall shrank to meet him, beating its arm against its side.

The reek of smoke and burnt cloth filled the stairway and followed him through the house.

There was a devil in the bathroom mirror. As he ran the cold water, his own eyes glared back at him, bloodshot, from a botched, inflamed mask. His hand in the water was a monster's, and a patch of the charred sleeve seemed welded to his skin. He saw what damage he had done to himself, and knew that he must get help.

The hallway was dark, except for what light spilled out from the bathroom door. He had quite forgotten the salvaged drawing, but he saw its pale shape now where it had fallen by the studio door, and despite everything he went back to get it.

When he turned on the lights he saw the studio stripped naked, an echoing space. The paper trembled in his hand. A whole corner of it was burned away, beside a cluster of graphite sketches — the fault lines of a shoulder, the flex of a wrist, an elbow. The reverse was a full, horizontal study — he knew the painting it had led to.

He could almost believe he remembered the day and the hour when he'd drawn that. The plain skirt she was wearing, the grey sweater that had moulded her breasts. She sat with her knees drawn under her on the couch, one hand combing back through her hair, lifting it from her downturned, reading face.

It was good.

He felt the old tremor, the twin desires again — for her in the flesh, and for the line and shade that might conjure that on the page. It was so confident, so minimal, so alive. "I must learn to draw again," he said, aloud, and then gave a weak, despairing laugh, because the pain was crawling through his shoulders now and he felt the skin of his forearm heaving and cracking in his sleeve.

He reeled against the door jamb, and made his way back along the hallway like a drunk man. He reached for a coat in the foyer, but it dragged from his hand as he closed the front door and he went down the street without it, fighting off delirium.

Then time was erased by place.

It was a pool by a ruined wharf, a backwater eddy clogged with debris from the river. Sometimes a light glanced across his face, sometimes there seemed to be figures looking down from the embankment. He was nudged by inert things that might have been other bodies. The water slapped against pilings and stone, and drowned voices came and went, confused and sorrowful.

He woke to find himself talking, in mid-sentence, with no idea what he had been saying. Two friends were staring at him from the bedside. The nearest one leaned towards him: "Welcome back to the world of the living," he said. The room was filled with impossible light. Behind a curtain an old voice wavered, confused and sorrowful.

Five days had gone by, they told him, and the healing could take a month or more.

A friend took him back to her home and tended to him with brisk affection. They had been lovers, briefly, years before, both part of a group who had known each other since college days and still met for drinks every Thursday in their old student haunt. He had visitors some evenings and a nurse came twice a week to change the dressings but his days alone in the house were a limbo of pain and lethargy.

The pain was a slumbering parasite that roused without warning, its ragged teeth latching into his hand. It was a snake that bit down and then swallowed, convulsively, in waves that surged back through his body and jolted his brain. As he clenched his eyes against it he saw a face, bitter and staring, a counterfeit of his own.

When the nurse peeled back the dressings, his hand lay between them on the kitchen table like a skinned animal's paw.

The pain stabbed through his sleep, in colours there were no names for. He came awake with the sheets, wet and cold, clinging to him, and his cry echoing in the room.

Perhaps his friend heard him; she did not say.

He never spoke about the pain, but he felt little pride in that. Standing by the french doors, flexing his bandaged fingers over and over as the nurse insisted he must, he felt lost and fraudulent in that bright, orderly home.

Every day new flowers appeared in the garden, and in the vases around the house. The tall lilac hedges shimmered with mauve and cream. Iridescent birds stalked on the grass with mad yellow eyes. The feeder under the apple tree was alive with smaller birds. But he watched the world through glass, as though all of his senses except sight were benumbed.

"You are so lucky," the nurse told him. "All your beautiful things. So lucky that your wife can go out to work while you get well again." He did not trouble to correct her. She worked at two jobs, sending money back to the children she had not seen for almost three years.

Each time she arrived she stood in the hallway, looking around and shaking her head in wondering approval in which he could see no trace of envy. She brought fluffy blue slippers with her, removing her boots at the door.

Her deft, plump fingers worked gently across his knuckles and up past his wrist, coaxing ointment into the blotched, peeling flesh. "I have seen worse things," she said. "I think soon it will all be better. Not pretty, but better." When she stroked his palm and flicked with her nails up to his fingertips, his skin would start tingling. The sensation grew stronger with each session.

One day, when he shuddered and tried to draw back his hand, her round face broke into a smile. She laughed as you might at a child you were tickling. "You see, now your hand is telling you how it is mending." And it was true. The pain was finally subduing itself, the venomous colours disappeared from his dreams, he began to sleep through the night.

A brown dove had made a nest in the creeper by his bedroom window. Each morning, he realized, the birds exchanged roles, brooding the two white eggs. He was almost a stranger to the natural world, but for his friend it was a passion. She knew the names of everything. When she got home from work, she went straight to the french doors, shedding her jacket and purse, and wandered through the garden, humming to herself, selecting flowers for her vases. She made soft kissing sounds that brought black and white birds down to feed from her hands. She had become like a bird herself, he thought – tidy, alert, untroubled.

It was hard to see in her the defiant, promiscuous girl she had been, the first of them all to get recognition, with her fierce, acrylic abstractions. One of those early paintings hung above the stairs. At first he had scarcely noticed it, but after a while he found himself stopping on the landing, outside her bedroom door, and staring across at it.

It had a perverse energy that ran from right to left as though a low waterfall had been turned on its side. And it *was* like water, the basic colour strands knitting together and unravelling, but with knots and details that broke the flow. As the picture grew more familiar he kept seeing those details as debris — the fragment of a boat's painted prow, a jagged tree limb, even a tan scoop of ribs that could have been from a boat too but suggested human or animal and challenged the whole scale of things. There were small ambushes of cadmiums, green and red, clotted and curdling, that leaked imperceptibly into the whole. It became a flood, for him — chaos in the act of forging its own kind of order.

She would have disdained any figurative notions, of course. She had always refused to give her paintings titles, saying that if you liked one enough to buy it you should be allowed to name it as well. One morning he realized that in the very foreground there was a counter current, that the painting's flow swung around, running 'east' in fast, narrow strokes. The painting was transformed by that. Each time that he stood there, it disclosed something new. There was envy mixed in with his growing admiration, and somehow he felt judged by the work, even as it drew him drew closer.

She had been twenty-three perhaps, when she made it, yet within a few years of that she had turned her back on it all. By the time of their brief involvement she had abandoned painting altogether, and refused to discuss it. When she'd accompanied him to openings and events she had introduced herself as his friend, a librarian. Yet he'd always felt she was impatient with his own work, even as his success mounted. Shamefully, it was his resentment at that that had led to their break up,

No one remembered her now, though there were paintings of hers in two big galleries that had ignored his own work.

They never spoke about painting. They spoke very little at all, and mostly during the evening meals that she prepared. She was waspishly funny about her colleagues and clients, yet she clearly enjoyed them and the balance she'd found between home and work. When the dishes were done she would go back to the garden or do house chores, and then read or listen to music till her bedtime. After the first few days, she had assumed he would fit into the schedules of her life.

But as he healed, as the dressings came off and he started to use his hand for everyday tasks; as the dove's eggs hatched and the two fluffball chicks became ravenous creatures, plunging their beaks into their overworked parents' mouths; and as his need for her lessened; he found himself growing more irritated by the day. What had at first been a haven at least, a place of kindness, was becoming foreign, indifferent.

She did almost everything for him, it was true, but it was in her own rhythms and order, and he felt increasingly as though he was invisible, shooed out of the way when she vacuumed or dusted, ignored except when he actually spoke to her. She seemed oblivious to his moods, or perhaps just refused to give in to them, to let her home be soured by resentments; and there was something, too, in her expressions — a quirk of the lips perhaps, or a lift of the brow – that suggested a knowing amusement that might actually be contempt.

It was a foolish argument.

"How can you just sit there, doing nothing?"

"I'm listening to the music."

"Yes, but that's all you're doing."

For him, music had always been the background when he was working, the hedge against an empty house when he wasn't."

"And what do *you* do all day, when I'm at work?"

That stung. Too many days had passed with him staring out at the window, loitering among the channels on the basement TV set, or leafing unfocussedly through the art books that were everywhere.

She reached to turn off the stereo. "Would you rather I was knitting?"

"Well reading, anyway, or talking."

"Would you want someone reading a book when she was supposed to be looking at one of your paintings?"

A taboo had been broken – his work, his career had never been discussed. He felt them turned against him.

"I wouldn't mind if they, if *she*, was listening to music."

"Then which would be the background – the music or your art?"

"Don't try to trap me with debating tricks."

She got up and went to the door. "I wouldn't insult Franz Schubert, or Lester Young, or Joni Mitchell, or anyone who'd given of themselves, by treating them as background."

At the foot of the stairs, she leaned back: "Especially to a pointless squabble about personal tastes."

He heard her footsteps overhead, then water running in the bathroom. He went down to the basement and switched on the television.

A French archaeologist was decoding a blood-crazed culture, their hilltop citadel long overwhelmed by the desert, the last ruler or high priest unearthed in his grave, clutching the stained, encrusted club with which he had slaughtered their captives.

He went softly upstairs, turning off all the lights, and as he passed her door he whispered, as if she might hear in her dreams, "I have to go home tomorrow."

He was woken early by cries and scuffles at his window, a black wing beating against the glass, a scatter of grey down.

A crow looked up at him from the dove's nest. Its beak gaped for an instant, the pearl that was a dove's eye rolling back on the sharp, blue tongue. As he shouted and flung the window open, the crow leaped back, with a last jab that dragged the fledgling out of the nest. Down on the lawn, two more crows were tearing at a lump of grey feathers.

He yelled out in fury, and it seemed to him that their cries mimicked him in defiance. He grabbed up his clothes, cursing himself and the crows, stumbling against the dresser as he pulled on his trousers.

Her bedroom door opened as he came out on the landing. She was barefoot, and one knee showed through the kimono which she held closed with both hands. Wide eyed, with her hair loose and tousled, she looked younger, waiflike.

His rage faltered. He lost his bearings completely. He felt in that instant that if he'd had anything left to offer they could become lovers again.

"What is it?"

He looked down. "The bastard crows," he muttered. "They've killed the young doves."

"Oh dear," she said. "That's too bad. I'll be down in a minute." Behind her as she turned he glimpsed a bright-patterned quilt, and on the wall beside her bed a large, almost monochrome painting.

Three crows flew up from the grass as he opened the french doors. Just to his right, beside the flower bed, a fledgling lay, one wing outstretched, its mouth gaping soundlessly, its eye socket raw. He could not stand this — he stepped down with his heel, revulsion rising to his throat as he felt the skull caving in. The crows were jeering in the apple tree. He wouldn't let them have the body. But when he bent to pick it up he stepped back in disgust.

She was standing at the french windows in her kimono, her hair tied back. She had a cup in each hand.

"They're mocking me."

"They're very intelligent birds."

"What does that say about intelligence?"

Her eyes were quite different from that girl's at the bedroom door; at once shrewd and gentle. She waited for him to take the cup from her.

"Let's leave it until tomorrow," she said. "Then I'll take you home. I've a lot to do today."

She went back inside and returned with a plastic bag. He watched her pick up the doves' bodies. The crows watched too, from the apple tree. "Get lost now," she told them, "you've had your fun." And they flew off in silence, disappearing over the lilacs.

"They only eat the eyes and brains," she said. "The rest would be wasted." There was no sign of the parent doves.

She left without eating breakfast. She wore jeans and sneakers, in place of her linen suit, with a light cotton smock like the ones the art students used. "Perhaps you should go out for a while,"she called back from the hall. "The spare key's on the hall stand. To the stores, I mean. Acclimatize yourself. I'll be back late afternoon."

He poured some more coffee. When he went to the fridge to get milk, the plastic bag with the doves' bodies lay on the top shelf.

Time had so dragged for him in the last months, years even, yet at the same time, strangely, it seemed to have evaporated. He had entered a state of inertia, broken by spasms of activity that went nowhere. It was almost midday before he roused himself and went upstairs. She was right, he should go out in the world, but the truth was, he was fearful. He badly needed his own space back, but he dreaded it too. The thought of his house dismayed him. Nothing would have changed.

He stopped at her bedroom door. Very quietly, as if she might be there, he opened it. It was a bright room, the bed beneath the window surrounded by space, pale walls, woven rugs on the hardwood floor, their pastels echoing the more vivid hues of her quilt. A vase of lilies on a pine dresser, another on the night table, beside some books and a blown-glass lamp. The flesh-scent of the lilies, and the faint perfume that was hers. A notebook lay against the pillows.

He stood by the bed and took in the painting. She had never signed her work, but there was her name, in the lower right corner. Without that, he'd never have guessed it was by her. Her last exhibition, just before his first years in New York, had tended towards quieter, flatter spaces, but nothing as calm and opaque as this. There was a date too — the year before he'd come back and they'd started their affair. In the apartment she rented back then, there had had not been a single piece of her work on the walls.

It had almost no movement at all, on the surface. Just the sense that a soft grey fabric was afloat above sandy shallows. Were the faint shadings towards mauve, here and there, signs that the fabric was absorbing the water and would drown? Or were they the last traces of moisture evaporating in the light, as the shawl drifted in? But of course there was nothing literal or figurative about it.

It had the stillness, the quiet deep texture of a late Rothko, but the hints of mad yellow beneath the fabric's edge (was it energy being subdued, or breaking out?) was like Clyfford Still, the only other one of that tribe that he'd ever felt drawn to. But it was hers — was it fair to look for comparisons as the critics inevitably did? He had always felt diminished when they did that to his own work — as though his originality had to be questioned. He sat on the bed and gazed at the canvas, for its own sake only. He reached out and touched it with a fingertip, just before her signature. He could not guess what kind of paint she had used, coarse in appearance, smooth to the touch.

He was as still as the painting.

It came to him that she had found her way to this, and that her quest had ended there. With ferocious clarity she had known she could go no further with her work, that to continue would be to repeat and to decline.

He bowed his head.

When he stood up, he did not smooth out his imprint on the quilt. He wanted her to know that he had trespassed and understood.

There was a small picture frame on her nightstand. A poor photograph of an infant, just born, in its mother's arms. Her face was not visible. He stared at the night stand. It was a Duncan Phyffe, and he was sure that he knew it. He knelt and felt behind the front right leg, just above the brass clawfoot. Yes, the gouged scar was there. This had been his mother's; he had sold it two years ago. The ironies crowded in on him. If she only knew...

He left the bedroom door ajar, and went straight downstairs, and out into the street.

The sunlit houses and trees to his right had a two dimensional clarity, while the sky behind them was a wall of Payne's grey. In that weird light he imagined that people would not see him, a time-traveller, a ghost. Two blocks away was a small strip mall. He went into the discount store there, as the first drops of rain hit the sidewalk and a sharp, grassy smell filled the air. By the time he had found some light cotton gloves, the rain was pelting down, and people hurried past the windows, shielding themselves as best they could from the downpour.

He asked if there was a coffee shop close by. The Chinese cashier glanced out at the rain and shrugged. "Maybe next door," she said. She did not look up as he she gave him his change; her eyes were fixed on his hand. He pulled on a glove as he went back outside.

It was a small Asian restaurant, just finishing a busy lunch hour, though several patrons were huddled in the doorway's shelter. Two girls, slight and agile, were clearing the tables, all smiles when they saw him. "Hello," sang the first one; "Welcome," sang the other.

"Could I just get a cup of coffee?"

"Yes, no problem. We make."

"Ah no," he said. "Don't make a fresh pot just for me."

"No pot — cup," she said. "Is easy. Sit please."

It was a sterile room, with formica tables and a linoleum-tiled floor. On the walls were prints of village scenes — thatched huts and banana palms, water buffalo and peasants with coolie hats and two-wheeled carts, variously combined against a backdrop of pointy green hills. Mass market trash, but perhaps it meant home to them. He chose a small table by the window, looking out on the street. The paper place mats came from the same atelier.

As he sat down, a wind gust banged a door somewhere. There was a scream of laughter from the kitchen, and the rain slapped in a full sheet against the window. The shapes and colours of the street blurred on the glass, and he remembered his wife, teetering on the old mill weir in Finisterre, clutching her pawnshop Leica. *Light swims upstream,* she'd shouted, *against the current*. He hadn't really listened, he'd been more concerned that she would fall into the millrace, but he understood now, watching the light as it trembled and stuttered but still held its own through the sluicing downpour.

He missed his *calepin*. It had been months since he had left his house, except to the local stores and the Thursday evenings, but before that he'd always carried the little sketchbook. It was a butterfly net to catch expressions, gestures, the tricks of light and perspective, but it was a shield too, and a companion. Without it he felt exposed, somehow, though the café was almost empty. He imagined a pencil between his gloved fingers and thumb. What would that be like?

The last customers were paying their bills, bracing themselves to dash out through the rain.

The old man at the counter, gaunt and diminutive in a bright yellow blouse, had the face of a sunken-cheeked Buddha. Each time he gave change, he folded his hands and bowed from the shoulder, and the lines of his face reached up as he smiled, into his brow.

It was a mask of impish kindness.

The coffee arrived. It was obviously instant coffee, made with milk. The girl waited and watched, and he tasted it out of politeness. To his surprise it was delicious – sweet, with a mild coconut aroma. "It's good," he said. She smiled and nodded, "Yes, good."

An older woman, with the broad face and stocky frame that the girls might inherit someday, came to the table. "First time we see you," she said, and set down a bowl before him. Her eyes flicked away from his glove. "Is Khmer goodie for you."

It was a tiny dumpling, in a pool of syrup. He picked it out with his left hand and ate while they watched. There was a custard inside, rich with coconut. "It's wonderful," he said. "Thank you. Could you lend me a pencil, or a pen?"

The woman brought him a ballpoint pen from the counter. Across the room, the old man bowed and smiled.

The other side of his place mat was blank. He pushed the bowl aside and started a sketch in the crude blue ink, between sips of his coffee. It was really quite easy. Different, though. Like the myth of Renoir, strapping the brushes to his crippled wrists. He became absorbed in the study. As he stole glances at the old man, he was vaguely aware that the rain had let up. The room was silent except for voices in the kitchen and the scraping of chairs as a girl rearranged things behind him.

She stopped at his shoulder and gasped, *"Pa-Oum!"* and when he turned with his finger to his lips, she covered her mouth with a giggle and hurried away. He could hear her talking rapidly in the kitchen.

He left the mat when he went to the counter, but the girl fetched it over, and the whole family came out from the kitchen. There was a young man too, with a girl's face, peering over their shoulders.

Their gaiety was communal. They passed the sketch around, exclaiming, even clapping. Somehow he was not embarrassed; their pleasure was infectious. Behind the old man the clock said that a whole hour and more had vanished. There was a calendar too. "What day is it?" he asked. "Is Tuesday," they chorused, laughing.

"Goodbye," they cried, as he went to the door. "We see you again next time." And the old man bowed and smiled, and the lines climbed into his brow, as they did on the place mat drawing.

It was nothing, but it was something. How long had it been since he'd walked smiling down a street? A woman pushing a stroller answered the smile as if it were meant for her, and her smile, reflected, lingered on his face as he walked back.

He was almost at his friend's gate when her car drew up.

She was smiling too.

"Just wait," she called. "I'm taking you somewhere."

He got into the car, and breathed in the same quiet perfume as in her bedroom.

When she returned, she had changed her smock for a brown, tailored jacket that subtly diminished her breasts. She was holding the bag with the dove carcasses.

"Are we going to feed the homeless?"

"You'll see," she said. "This is your payback for all my tender care."

There was music playing, piano and violin, when she started the engine.

"Well, I know better than to talk while you're listening."

She laughed. "Touché. I can turn it off if you like."

"No, it's fine."

She drove through slow traffic, north past the malls and freeways, beyond the old city limits. Here and there among the split level suburban homes a brick farmhouse stood out, with its high dormer windows. There were old sugar maples too, from a time before.

He watched her, as she drove: her chin lifted, the hint of a smile on her lips.

She glanced over. "What do you see?"

"Your jawline, I've always loved jawlines. They're my favourite limbs."

She laughed again. "Pick on someone younger."

"I was thinking that as you get older you start to love flesh in its failure, because the failure is actually knowledge, experience. There's something *kind* about it."

"Hmm. That's very eloquent, but it's also crushing and I wish you'd stop staring. I'm sensitive about my poor neck."

"Your neck is beautiful."

"Kind?"

"Very kind."

She turned off the highway, onto a switchback exit.

"'*Limbs*'," she said. "You're becoming your old self again," and pulled into a parking lot.

He looked up at the sign. "The zoo? What's this about?"

"Just humour me," she said.

They walked towards the turnstile. She held the bag with the doves close to her side.

"I'd have thought you hated zoos."

"I do," she said, "and I have a season's pass."

A high, fluting call came from somewhere inside the grounds. She turned towards him. "*We think caged birds sing, when indeed they cry.*"

The man at the ticket booth waved them through. "We close in an hour, go ahead."

In the big enclosure that faced them there were zebras and antelopes, and beyond the small lake, giraffes.

"We go this way," she said.

Resistance flared up in him. "No," he said. "I can't think why you've brought me here, but I've no interest in watching you feed your pet anaconda or whatever it is. You go on. I'll walk around by myself."

She looked only amused. "Suit yourself," she said. "I'll meet you back here then," and she set off towards the rank of high cages to their left, moving like a woman half her age.

The place was almost deserted. He stood at the enclosure's rail, watching the African creatures move under Canadian trees. He imagined winter.

There was such irony in seeing the ducks and geese flying in and out of the enclosure, the small birds foraging around the zebra's hooves, the squirrels and chipmunks scavenging on both sides of the fence. There was a huge nest in a solitary maple by the lake. Swallows were flying everywhere, close to the ground.

He went across to the cages. In the first, a lion lay in absolute sloth by its bars, and he thought of the two Delacroix in the Louvre, the lion hunted, the lion attacking the riders. The energy of those, against this squalid inertia.

The Delacroix stayed with him as he walked off. At twenty-five he had fallen under that spell, the magical triumph of paint over contour. Success had followed, and then the slow procession of betrayals, of himself, of others . . .

There were alleys between the cages, leading to smaller enclosures. He wandered, scarcely noticing the animals that he passed; they just seemed without presence – at once caged in and surrounded with naked space. A woman was pulling the shutters down on a concession booth, and he went into the washroom beside it. There was a chalkboard above the urinals, to discourage graffiti. In precise, small lettering someone had written:

Animals share with us the privilege of having a soul – Pythagoras

below that was scrawled:

next time around you might be a cockroach

He stepped out into the sunlight and walked back towards the African field. It was surely almost time to leave. He looked down the line of cages to see if she was waiting, and then he felt eyes upon him.

It was a small cage, with a low hutch at its rear, and a cat's face was glaring out at him from the darkness. He went closer. *Canadian Lynx* the sign read, and below that

maimed by an illegal leghold trap,
this native of the northern forests
could not be returned to the wild

He had never seen such concentrated rage as he did in those topaz eyes. Here was energy, a refusal to say *I am helpless*. It was proud, and murderous.

They stared at each other. On an impulse he could not have put words to, he pulled off his glove and held up his hand to the bars. He saw it as if for the first time, with a stranger's eye: waxen and smooth, without pores or knuckle-lines, just the livid ridges that traced his veins, as they did half way up his forearm. As a hand it was a travesty, but as an object, a creature, it had a kind of beauty. He imagined it with pale webs between the fingers.

The air reeked of tomcat. He stared at his hand. It seemed to him that the lynx was watching it too.

"I wondered if you might find him. He's implacable, isn't he?"

He had not been aware of her till she spoke.

"You're sure it's a he?"

She ignored that. "If you had to find a name for him, what would it be?"

He looked back at the unflinching cat's eyes.

"Remorse," he said.

"That's very good," she said. "For me he's always been Mephistopheles."

They watched together. The lynx's stare defied them both — not even fierce now, indifferent rather, as if they merely impeded his horizon.

"You could paint him," she said. "You have that ability."

It was the second breach of their taboo, and he felt the judgment in her words.

"Why don't *you*? "he retorted.

"Oh," she said quietly, her eyes still fixed on the lynx's face. "I've tried. I can't make it work, do him justice."

"You're painting?"

She gave a quick, direct look. "It's what I do on winter evenings," she said. "I decided to show you before you leave." She took his arm, and drew him away from the cage. "That's why I brought you here."

"But when did you start painting again?"

"A couple of years ago." She laughed, and hurried him on. "When I gave up on men."

They joined the small crowd that was streaming out through the gate.

He supposed that those people would see them as a couple. This small, alert woman, with keen features and iron grey hair, and himself, no doubt clumsy beside her in his loose clothes, and a face — what would they see there? Though he shaved every morning, when had he last really studied his face? He couldn't paint it if he tried. Yet once the self-portrait had been his ambition. The Otto Dix in Detroit, the three Stanley Spencers in England – their fearless self-scrutiny, the fascinated self-love – he had promised them that he would do as well, and except for a few early sketches it had come to nothing. Like so many promises.

All the traffic was leaving the city, and the drive back was quick.

"We'll eat takeout," she said. "Then I'll show you my work. There's a new Cambodian place round the corner; it's very good."

"I think I had coffee there this afternoon."

"Well the food's great," she said, "and they're dear people."

He smiled at the recollection, but when she drew up by the café he said he'd rather walk back.

"That should time out well. There's wine in the fridge, if you feel like opening it."

He found the table already laid, with wine glasses and chopsticks, and a vase of many-coloured sweet peas whose scent filled the kitchen. The wine was a *Pouilly-Fumé*. He used to buy it by the case; she must have remembered.

He tried to match her gaiety over their meal, sensing in it her relief at seeing him gone. The food was new to him, subtly different from Thai cooking. "I did a sketch of the old man," he told her. "I couldn't resist his face."

"They're not family, you know." She leaned back in her chair, and told him the story. "He found them in a refugee camp and adopted them, to get them out. He'd lost all three generations of his own family, and their father had been killed too, and the eldest son."

"They seemed so happy."

"Anything I could say to that would be banal." She refilled her glass and got up. "Bring your wine," she said. "Dutch courage in my case."

He followed her up the stairs, to the landing. She unlocked a door that he had assumed was a third bedroom. It was a small, tidy studio, with a drawing board set at an acute angle. She handed him her glass and went to a tall corner cabinet. "This is in confidence, okay? I mean that."

There were photographs on one wall, a dozen close-ups of animal faces, but it was the drawing across the room that riveted him. It was big, a forcefully modelled image of her younger self, her face in repose but full of uncertainty, her lips slightly parted, the volumes of cheek and neck exquisitely rendered, the brow conjured with minimal strokes. It was masterful.

"Who did this?"

"Oh for god's sake," she said. "What's wrong with you?" She was laying out small paintings on the drawing board. "*You* drew it."

He stepped closer to the drawing. Had it really meant so little then, that he had forgotten it? He stared with incredulous envy.

"We're here to see *my* work," she said. "So give me my glass and get on with it."

She went and leaned by the window.

They were the last things he could have expected. Each picture was of an animal's eye. The skin surrounds and the naked lids were painted in minute, textured detail, but the irises imploded into a chaos of tropical storm, or scorched earth, with nightmare gestures of mouths and nostrils and tormented limbs.

He bent close to one of the paintings. "You must have thinned down your oils to within an inch of their lives."

"No, it's egg tempera, mostly. I love it. It dries so quickly. You can do layer upon layer."

She took the paintings and replaced them with three more. For a moment her eyes met his — there was a child in their brown depths, praying for approval.

He turned away and went over to the window. "The emotions seem human to me," he said. "You've made them half human."

She looked down at the paintings. "How else could I inhabit that pain?"

"I don't know that it's pain," he said. "Most of them were born in captivity, that's all they know."

"But that's the worst pain of all," she said. "Not understanding your dreams."

She shook her head, and gathered the paintings together.

"No listen," he said. "Please. I'm not carping; I just can't find the right words. *Please.*"

She turned back to face him.

"They're exquisite and brutal," he said. "They're amazing. I'm frightened by them, by their skill as much as their subject, and I'm full of an envy you could never guess at."

She closed the cabinet door. "Let's go down and get a drink," she said.

They sat by the french windows, a bottle of cognac between them, and she talked about her first visit to the zoo, an unwilling tagalong with her sister's grandchildren. "I hadn't felt so incapably sad for years," she told him.

"What will you do with them? Who's seen them?"

"No one but you. And it's staying that way."

"And why me?"

She shrugged. "I don't know, to be honest. Just –" She shrugged again.

"But they're so good. And you do them just for their own sake? As if it were a hobby?"

"There's enough art out there, good and bad," she said. "And the world's become a shit hole. If we don't work for the angels and the ancestors, there's no point really."

They sat in silence for a while. "Anyway," she said, "I'm going to bed. I'll take you home in the morning."

She left the bottle on the coffee table. "Goodnight" she called, from the foot of the stairs.

"I owe you an apology."

"One of many," she said, with complete friendliness. "You're forgiven."

She knocked on his bedroom door in the morning. "We'll have to hurry; I have a meeting at nine."

As they drove off she said, "There's milk and juice in your fridge, and croissants in the bin. Coffee and tea on the counter and a few other things. I'll take you shopping on Saturday for anything you need."

A cold spasm went through him.

"You've been in my house?"

"Well of course, it had to be locked up – here are your keys, by the way. How did you think I got your clothes and stuff?"

All he could think of was her seeing the bare walls, the rooms stripped of rugs and furniture, where once there had been elegance. No one had been in his house for two years. He leaned his head against the window, numb with shame.

"Front door or back?" she asked, at the top of his street.

"Back, I guess."

She parked by the gate, and got his bag from the trunk. In her librarian suit, she was someone else altogether.

She kissed him on the cheek. "I'll pick you up tomorrow," she said. "Around seven. But I'll call ahead.

"And this is from all of us." She thrust an envelope into his hand and went back to the car.

He stood irresolute at the gate as she drove away, tooting her horn at the end of the lane.

Everything felt unreal. The garden path, and the grey crater of the firepit. The steps where he had staggered that night, on fire. It was someone else's story. Coming up the stairwell, into the familiar smell of the place, he was a ghost in his own home.

He dropped his bag and went into the studio. The drawing he had saved from the fire had been pinned up, high on the easel. He sat on the couch, and closed his eyes. His blood knocked slowly at his ear drums.

An hour might have passed. The envelope she had given him fell from his hand, and brought him back to himself. After a minute, he tore it open. It was full of money, hundreds of dollars. There was a card, a reproduction of one of his paintings. On the back — *Keep the faith, we love you.*

He cried out, loud in the bare room.

Was his penury common knowledge then? He had never shown it to them. His clothes were old, but they were good, expensive things he had bought in the glory days. How long had they been pitying him?

The thought of them knowing, of talking about him, was unbearable.

He went walking from room to room, back and forth, trying to shed the humiliation. Hadn't he pitied them, too, at times, for their lost dreams and compromised lives? In ten years or less they would all be retiring, with comfortable pensions and fewer regrets than his own.

And they might pity him, but they were not gloating. Nor had they shown any envy when he was aloft. They had welcomed him back with delight, he remembered, when he'd turned up alone one Thursday evening after years in more glamorous circles. Even then, they had shown more grace than he had.

And they'd given him cash now, he knew, so that he could not ignore a cheque.

He was not ready to face them.

So when she called, the next evening, he did not pick up the phone. He stood in the kitchen and listened to the answering machine: "I'm quite sure you're there," her voice said, "and I'm coming to pick you up."

He shaved quickly and went out down the backstairs, but she appeared at the gate and came up the path to meet him. Her hand reached out. "Come on," she said. "Don't be proud."

He found himself weeping. "You don't know," he sobbed. "You have no idea. The house isn't mine any more, I owe money, nothing sells." He could not look at her. "It's hopeless. I've been living on nothing for almost ten years."

She took him in her arms. The gentleness in her that he had forgotten was there. She kissed his mouth softly but he flinched away, staring up through the pear tree's branches as if that might drain the misery back into hiding.

"You should have told us," she said. "Come on now. We'll work something out."

She drove in silence, holding his hand the whole way.

They walked in through the lounge. The bartender waved, and made a smiling *namaste* bow. Familiar voices were loud already in the back room

It might have been tact, or perhaps just the heat of their usual debate, disagreeing on principle, laughing, denouncing. Art, politics, food. They greeted him casually, made room at the table, and went on with their jousting.

An American painter had just died, after years of schizophrenic withdrawal. The Whitney was planning a retrospective.

Was she a fraud, a victim, a sell-out, a genius?

"I've got a painting of hers somewhere," he said.

There was a silence. His friends looked at him, and at each other.

"Somewhere?" one said.

"It's in my basement, I think. I'd forgotten about it."

"Have you any idea what it would be worth?"

There was another silence. All eyes were on him. A hand reached for his under the table.

One of them stood up and raised his glass. "Well, shall we go and see it?"

They were back in their student days. Illicit bottles were coaxed from the bartender, and within minutes four cars were heading in convoy across the city. She squeezed his hand as they drove off. "Some prayers are answered," she said. "How on earth did you come by her painting?"

"We had a joint show in New York. Back in the day."

"Were you lovers?"

"Far from it," he said. "I hardly knew her. We just had the same gallery."

They had not really cared for each other's work, but they'd traded paintings at the end of the show. It was what you did in those days.

The tribe took over his house like a whirlwind, finding glasses and chairs for themselves and sprawling around in his studio. He turned on the kitchen radio to a jazz station, loud enough to carry down the hall. When he went in, someone had slid the mercy envelope under the couch.

"Well?" "We're waiting." "Go get it!"

He counted mechanically the eleven steps down to the basement, as he always did, but he paused with his hand on the dark room door. It had been a long time. When he turned on the light, it flashed once and went dead. He felt for the hanging cord, and the safelight came on, making a cave of the place with its dim red glow. The dome of his wife's old enlarger gleamed there, and he breathed in the ghosts of old chemicals. Her developing trays were stacked on the shelves, with dusty hypo bottles and cartons of paper. The place was a crypt.

The painting was propped against the wall, perhaps two feet square and still in the paper wrapping he had brought it home in. Beside it was the bag that his grandad, the country doctor, had carried all his life. The black initials stamped on its side, the same as his own. If he opened it there'd be those tubes of oil paint, the cloth wrap of brushes, that had not seen the light in twenty-five years.

He heard feet on the basement steps. "You okay down there?"

"Yes, I'm coming," he shouted. "I'll be up right away."

He felt totally shy when he brought in the package. Their faces were a study, as he unwrapped it. And there it was – geometric yet skewed, like a mutant honeycomb, its cells on the verge of dissolution, with a vaguely sinister brown ochre bloom. An uneven fissure was tearing its way through the structure.

"It's the Fall of the House of Usher," someone said.

And one of the others, "There's writing on the back."

In conté she'd written:

toujours gai, kid
we sow what we reap

He hadn't known it was there.

"Is that really deep, or completely meaningless?"

"Worth an extra million, at least."

"Put it on the easel."

He set it up, and turned the easel spots on. His own drawing was half-covered by it.

One of his friends, the art director with an advertising firm, went out and talked on the phone. Ten minutes later his son appeared with two bottles of Dom Pérignon. It became a real party, full of argument, reminiscence, singing too. But each one of them, from time to time, looked quietly at the painting, and thought his or her own thoughts.

It did not go late; they were all working people, and student stamina was far in the past. He knelt down and retrieved the envelope. "I won't need this now, I guess," he announced. "But it means more to me now, for some reason, than it did before." He felt the booze slurring his words and his eyes were wet, but he staggered as he got up and was saved by their laughter. "You can pay for our Thursday bills, till it runs out," the art director said, and then, taking him aside: "I made a call to some people. They'll be in touch tomorrow. You can trust them"

He stood at the door, watching the cars drive away. His old lover was tidying things in the kitchen. He went in and rescued a half-full glass of champagne before she could pour it down the sink. She wiped her hands. "What will you do now?" she asked.

"I think you should stay."

She patted his arm. "You're quite drunk," she said. "Try to drink some water before you sleep."

He took his glass back to the studio and confronted the painting. "I owe you my freedom, Madame," he said, with a courtly flourish. "Your gift from the grave. *Toujours gai.*" Then he took it down and propped it against the easel's foot.

"But I owe you more," he told the drawing, "and I will repay."

He would begin at once. He drained the glass and made his way to the basement door. At the sixth step he staggered and almost fell, sliding against the wall the rest of the way down. The dark room was eerie, and the black bag much heavier than he expected. He lugged it up the stairs, crooning to it as if it were a child or a cat, all the way to the studio.

He held it up to the drawing.

"I believe you know each other," he said.

He set it down on the floor and stepped back. It was a fine still-life arrangement – the black bag, his initials, the painting, his drawing, the easel.

He was so drunk. He went to the couch and fell back on it, laughing.

The telephone woke him, and he vaguely heard a man's voice leaving a message. The room smelled of smoke and wine, and his mouth was parched. When he sat up, pain flared through his temples. The easel spots were still on. He went to the kitchen and drank some water, then threw himself down on his bed. The phone woke him again. It was the fine-art auction house. "Please call us," the voice said, and gave a number. "We heard about your find and we'd like to talk with you."

He made coffee and called them back. They would come right away. "Just give me an hour," he said. He showered and shaved, and closed all the doors but the studio's.

There were three of them, two thirty-year-olds in expensive suits and a tall woman in her fifties who stood back and watched. They would auction it in their New York house, they said. When they gave their estimate, their suggested reserve price, he was speechless. It was grotesque.

"Would you give me an advance," he asked, "if I let you handle it?"

The woman laughed. "Just name it," she said, and held out her hand.

They drove him to their office, and then to their bank. As he walked to the main branch of his own bank, he imagined the street as a movie set. He could hear the music.

He felt time speeding up, and he let it take hold of him. He paid bills, bought clothes, booked a flight, and left one phone message: *"I'm going to Paris. My keys are under the bottom step. That money's in the kitchen. Thank you for everything."*

It was a night flight, and almost empty. He had three seats to himself. Across the aisle a girl sat by the window, and he watched as she dealt with the garrulous man in the aisle seat. She got up and went back to the washroom, and they shared a complicit smile, but though there were several empty rows, she was too kind-hearted, or well brought up, to offend the man. She took refuge in sleep.

There was nothing so trusting and innocent as a young sleeper. He thought of sketching her, but it would be as much a cliché as the thought. A generic young blonde, her hair, clothes, body type even in the style of her time. Through the dark window that framed her profile, the wing lights beat steadily, and he fell asleep.

The girl came out through customs as he did and they stood together at the baggage carousel. "I'm meeting my boyfriend," she told him. "We're going down to Provence for a month. I'm so excited. And you?"

"Well, retracing my steps, really."

"Oh fun," she said. "What are you hoping to find?"

He laughed, there was mischief and irony in those clear young eyes.

The carousel started turning. The black doctor's bag was one of the first down the chute. As he reached for it, she asked if he needed a hand, and then she flushed.

"I'm fine," he said. "The glove's aesthetic, not prosthetic."

"Sorry, anyway," she said. "And I love your bag."

Her eyes lit up, looking beyond him to the glass doors. She waved and leaped up and down, and then laughed with him at her giddiness. "There he is," she said. "And here's my bag." It was a backpack, almost as tall as she was. "I think you're the one that needs – well, help," he said, but she was more than capable.

"Good luck on your backtrack," she said, with the kindest look he'd ever seen on a young face. He watched her skip through the doors, drop her pack and get swung up in her boyfriend's arms.

He retrieved his other bag and followed the crowd to the metro. A train left the station just as he got there, and the girl was at a window, waving to him. He took it as a good omen.

He went straight to the old territory, upscale now and expensive beyond anything they could have imagined or afforded. The smell of the narrow streets was unchanged, though – the enchanting compound of Gitanes, spilled wine, ripe peaches, slow drains, with pockets of gaudy perfumes and the low tainted breath of the river.

He found an apartment quickly, because he could afford it. It was the second floor of a four-story *immeuble,* with a narrow entry hall and a huge, east-facing living room. It was perfect – he could keep it bare and primitive, but there was central heating now, in place of the old charcoal stove.

He bought a new bed, but for everything else he raided the flea markets. His prize was the old couch. It was common enough, of its period, but he let himself believe that it was the one from the old apartment. When it was delivered he believed it even more. He set it against the wall, and pinned the drawing above it.

Much had changed, but much was the same, too. The tiny *marchand de couleurs* was still there, on the street where they'd lived, with the same proprietor, now a withered, cantankerous old man. He bought watercolours and paper, and a student easel, and walked back with them past their old building. Behind those shutters on the third floor, did his ghosts ever stir? Did they meddle with people's dreams?

He carried a sketch pad everywhere, but he did not work in the way that he'd promised himself. He was re-entering a world. The language he had never quite lost came back as he chatted with shopkeeepers and waiters; he even dreamed in it one night. He spent most days in the galleries and museums, with such different eyes now. Things he had loved before seemed either overblown or too easy. He kept looking for things to fall in love with.

The cafés were still irresistible, though. Each table, it seemed, in his quartier was a tableau vivant, with a secret. One night he watched three figures caught up in a story that would not let him go. Complicit they might be, but there was a Judas among them, and he could not decide which it was. He took out his sketchbook.

At the heart was the woman's face, still beautiful and in the glory of power. The young man beside her, not much more than a boy, eyes brilliant and gauche with desire that may already have been gratified, and her husband's face leaning in, handsome and brutal, his hand toying with her hair where her neck met her shoulders, as they all drank together and ate voraciously, and kept laughing.

The sketch came together, deft and unkind, just this side of caricature. He wished he'd used ink and wash – it was almost a Daumier. Might he actually work it up into a painting? He found a nub of conté in his pocket, and started shading – hints for what he might do on a larger scale. He was smiling to himself. Those faces, shaped by appetite and deceit, leaned in together and composed their own frame. The hands were so treacherous, the mouths and eyes so avid.

He looked up. The husband was standing there, pointing towards the drawing. He drew the sketchpad away but the man reached down and tore the sheet lose. What would happen now? Would that big hand, with its gold watch and bracelet and dark-haired knuckles, swoop down and grab him up by his shirt collar? Or would the drawing simply get crumpled or torn up and thrown in his face?

A grim smile formed instead on the big man's lips. "*Bene, molto bene*," he said, and went back with the drawing to his table. The woman was not pleased, as she should not have been, and the young man looked indignant and scared at the same time. The husband sat back, enjoying. He let out a savage laugh and slapped the table. He did not care at all what the drawing had made of him

The woman glared across the room, and gathered up her purse. The three of them stood and prepared to leave. He started up too, but the husband gestured to him to stay seated, and snapped his fingers for a waiter. They left without looking back. The waiter came to his table a minute later, poker faced, and set down a glass of Armagnac. On the saucer beside it was a banknote. It was almost a whole month's rent.

He raised his glass to the shade of Daumier.

"*Vous parlez Anglais monsieur*?"

He nodded. It was a young American he'd seen earlier that day in Petite Boucherie, pointing things out to his wife, trying a little too hard to enjoy their adventure.

"We're on our honeymoon, and I'd really like you to draw my wife. I saw what that other man gave you and – "

"What can you afford?"

Even that seemed excessive to him, but he said "All right."

She was pretty, and loved, but all she wanted was to be back at home. His drawing flattered her, but he got all that into her eyes, for them to recognise down the road, if the drawing survived.

They were thrilled with it, though, and he wandered home by a roundabout route, replaying the evening. It was surely a sign. He'd been playing the student; now he'd found a more interesting role, or it had found him.

His beard came in white. He bought clothes that suggested years of shabby defiance. There was money enough to be made, sketching tourists on the *terrasses,* that he could have lived on that alone.

He'd look in shop windows as he passed, and see a character reflected, out of a film. He could hear the music. He could be this person for ever.

In the winter, there were fewer tourists in the indoor cafés, but he sketched for his own sake too – giving his drawings away to local customers, finding his place in the community.

He heard from the auction house that the painting had sold, well above their estimate, to a tycoon in Sweden. Thanks to a dead, mad painter, he was a millionaire several times over.

He chose not to think about it. It was someone else's story.

Spring came and the tourists were back. He was sketching a Japanese couple, catching the woman's face from two angles, reflected in her seat by the brasserie window.

A girl sat down at the table beside him. She leaned closer to look at his drawing.

"She is not so beautiful."

"She is to him," he said, without looking up.

He was used to such distractions. He went on with his drawing.

When he was finished, and the couple stood holding it, smiling, she started to applaud. He looked over, in irritation. It was the girl from the plane.

"Oh," he said, "Hi. Remember me?"

She looked puzzled.

"From the plane."

She shrugged.

He took his payment, and shook hands with the tourists, then turned back to the girl.

"We were on the same flight from Toronto last year."

"Ah, Canada," she said. "I was in Halifax one time. It is a nice town enough, but it rainèd all the time. Toronto I don't know."

He smiled at her affected accent. "Come on now, don't pretend."

"I never pretend. What is the use of it?" She pushed his sketch pad towards him. "Now please, you will draw me too."

"Where's your boyfriend?"

"Boyfriend? No, there is no one. Perhaps you will be my boyfriend?"

He laughed, and shook his head at her foolishness.

She took a sip of her wine, and leaned backwards. "I will look straight at you, yes?"

"Whatever you want," he said.

He decided on pen and ink. It would be quick, accurate, and good enough.

"I am ready now," she said. "I will be so still for you."

The voice seemed low, and the accent actually credible. Yet it was the same girl, there could be no mistake.

He started to work, and her eyes upon his did not flinch. When she reached for her glass, her face did not move. The blue eyes had a child's clarity, yet they were scarcely innocent. Could it really be someone else?

The pen made its quick whipping strokes on the paper.

"I want to know," he said. "Are you playing a part? I would understand that, believe me."

She shook her head slightly, twice, with no change of expression.

The work was involving him now. He kept leaning forward, *looking,* then back to the drawing. Almost imperceptibly he was tightening the lips, making the eye sockets deeper, as though the skull was floating up through her skin. Now he wished he had chosen graphite instead.

He dipped his left forefinger into her wine glass and made a light wash down the side of her face, across the exquisite clavicle.

"There." He turned the pad around. She drew it towards her, and gazed intently, sipping at her wine, expressionless.

"It is magic, what you do."

"Oh no," he said. "No it isn't. It's only a likeness," wishing, though, that he could have done more with it.

She looked sharply at him, then back to the drawing. "No," she said. "It is the something in her eyes that I think even you do not understand."

She could not be the Canadian girl. He stared at her, and she met his eyes without challenge.

Her hand reached over, and tugged at the cuff of his glove. He recoiled, but she kept tight hold and it came off completely.

She gasped. "It is beautiful. Like a dragon." Her face was alight with pleasure. "I think perhaps that angels have dragons' hands."

"I am no angel."

She sniffed contemptuously, and dropped his glove on the drawing. "You do not know this. Now please, I would like to go walking with you." She took his hand. "Is okay?"

He felt time take hold of him again. He left the glove on the table and they walked hand in hand along back streets and alleys, towards the river. He watched her face, the shadows changing it each time they passed a streetlight. She swung his arm, walking with a lilt that reminded him of his age, yet it was sweet, this, walking at night with a young girl by the Seine.

They passed the water steps where Arab musicians were playing and singing to their own small crowd, and stopped under a solitary light, as the embankment curved inwards above a boat dock.

"The river is so sad," she said. "I think every river must be sad."

"Is there a river where you come from?"

"Oh yes, a *very* sad river. But it saved my life."

"And where is that?"

"Nowhere with a name," she said. "You do not want to know. Sometimes we have been swallowed up – *snap* – in one whole piece, sometimes we are two, three countries." She let go of his hand and leaned over the parapet. *"Mon pays n'existe pas!"* she shouted to the river.

The water below them rocked and swirled in the dim light. You could imagine faces down there, voices too. He felt the urge to pull her to him, to kiss her.

"Where do you live now?" he whispered.

She turned and looked up at him, as though she were waiting for the kiss. "I live with friends most times, here and there." She took his hand again. "It is so cold, your dragon's hand. It is as sad and cold as the river I think."

She brought the hand close to her lips and breathed out on it, softly, tracing his fingers. "Perhaps you will have me to live with you now? For a small time at least?"

Did she mean it?

"I don't even know your name."

"Oh that," she said. She moved off, tugging at his arm. "I think when you know me more than this girl you walk with beside the river, you can give me a name. So then I will find a name for you also."

When they reached his building she ran up the stairs before him, stopping at each door. "Is this one? This one?" When he let her inside, she roamed through the place, exclaiming, questioning. "We will be happy here," she said, and went over to the couch. She leaned her knees against it and looked at the drawing. "This is good."

He laughed, "Well, thank you."

"You must not laugh," she said. "I can know what is good. You like it also, or it would not be there."

"I do," he said. "It's what I want to live up to."

"Live up to? Sometimes I must guess what you are telling me."

"I drew that a long time ago," he said. "I am not as good as I was then."

"You are very good," she said. "I think you are better than good."

She went into the bedroom, then leaned from the doorway. "Come and sit with me on the bed."

He felt shy, and awkward. It was three years since he'd been with a woman.

She went into the bathroom, and he heard her rummaging in the drawers and cabinet. When she came back she was wearing only a t-shirt. She was holding his paper scissors. He stared at her legs.

"That hairy face," she said. "Very silly. I will not kiss a sheep."

"Just wait now," he said. "My beard is part of who I am."

"It is who you pretend you are. You are very handsome inside all that."

He leaned against the headboard, and she straddled him, tilting his head back roughly as she began to snip.

"Delilah," he said, very conscious of her body against him.

"Ah, I know that story." She'd made a hammock with her T-shirt, catching the curls and shreds of his beard. Her concentration was like a painter's. "I think that one day they will find in a cave somewhere the other side of that story."

She must have been able to feel his arousal, but she ignored it.

"You have had many women, you, in your life?"

"Not so many."

"You are married I think?"

"I was. A long time ago. She has a family now, with someone else."

She stopped cutting for a moment.

"You are sad about that?"

"Sad yes – guilty, mostly."

"Ach, that." She tilted his head to one side. His hands lay on her thighs now. "It must be a new life each time," she said. "I have had many lives, and see how young I am still."

She brushed the back of her hand along his jawline.

"Well, you have me now," she said. "For a small time at least."

She climbed off the bed, and he saw her nakedness up to her waist. She came back from the bathroom with his shaving mirror, and sat beside him, holding it. His reflection and her face were side by side, watching. She was so young, so beautiful.

She put down the mirror. "Your face is very harsh now, of course," she said. "But you are not a sheep any more. So now I can kiss you."

For all her energy and wilfulness, she was a curiously passive lover, expressing her pleasures with small, indrawn whimpers. She fell asleep like a child, holding his hand to her breast, and he watched for a long time, thinking of the same face against the plane's window, the wing lights flashing, his new life a leap in the dark.

She woke him, with coffee and croissants from the boulangerie at the corner. His stubble was catching on the pillow, and he was eager to shave. He looked at himself in the little mirror — no longer the old sidewalk artist.

She was standing by the couch looking again at the drawing.

"So who is this girl?" she said. "This is a beautiful woman, so you must have loved her, no?"

"It's my wife."

"You have kept the *canapé*, all this time? You had it in Canada, and back again?"

"I found it in the *marché aux puces*. It might be the same one, though."

"I think so too."

He went and held her. "Come back to bed."

"No, I am going out now. It is important." She held his face in both hands. "Oh I like how I have made you to look."

She was still not back by mid-afternoon. He was completely on edge. He left the door unlocked and went out, and walked and sat in cafés, praying that she had not vanished, unable to think about anything but her.

When he came home she was sitting with a book on the couch, in exactly the pose of the drawing. Her skirt and sweater matched the ones that his wife used to wear. He felt blasphemy, relief, and then glad amazement.

"Now you make the first drawing," she said, looking up from the book. "Then I think we will make love, over and over."

It became a ritual, their whole life was constructed of rituals, yet there were always surprises. In their long evening walks, exploring new back lanes and stairways, she would dart off and find something he would never have noticed, or valued, and make it precious in his eyes.

Like him, she haunted the *brocantes* and flea markets, but with a better eye. She came back once with an ancient mirror, its silvering half-perished into tendrils that could have been leaf veins, or an estuary. She hung it in the hallway, in the shadows, but when you looked in it, the light from the big room made your face appear, the stems of dark silver branching through your reflection.

She loved to sit cross-legged on the floor or the bed, wearing one of his shirts, and ask for a story. She listened with an amusement that bordered on mockery, yet she was in awe of the things that he knew, and smiled as if she had discovered a treasure trove. He found himself searching his memory, while he worked, for stories he could share when they stopped for the day and she'd reach for the story shirt.

She might disappear, though, for two or three days at a time, without notice. After one fearful spell, when he dreamed she was not coming back, he demanded again where she went.

"With my friends, like I have told you — they are too young for you."

"You mean I'm too old for them."

She spun away, with a short, angry laugh. "I mean what I say."

She never asked for money, but she took what he gave her, and spent on whatever she wished. They never ate at home; she had no interest in cooking, or in anything domestic. Yet she could not bear to have a cupboard left open. Sometimes she got up in the night to make sure they all were closed.

He fell more in love every day. It might have seemed hopeless, ridiculous even, except for his work.

He drew her on the couch, in that pose, a dozen times. He tried line and wash, then a watercolour that pleased them both. He studied and sketched her for hours every day. She could hold any pose, in a kind of trance, without tiring. She would throw off her clothes whenever he asked, but the moment she sensed desire in his eyes, she would cover herself. "There's no difference," he told her. "Tell lies to yourself if you want," she said. "Not to me, please." There was something unreachable. And there were ambushes, too.

He found her in the bathroom one day, with the doctor's bag open on the floor, and the taps running.

She saw him in the mirror. "Don't be angry," she said, "I am making loose these lids, they are so hard."

"I'm not ready for that," he said, and grabbed up the bag. "You shouldn't have done this."

She turned around, a wrinkled tube of magenta in one hand, a squeezed out worm of it on her forefinger. "It is so juicy," she said, "and the smell, I love it. What is the problem you have now?"

She turned back to the mirror and daubed thick lines on her cheeks and brow. "Then I paint myself, if you will not."

"I was no good," he said.

"I do not believe."

"It's true. I was slick, that's all."

"Slick?"

"Lazy, easy, like the drawings I did in the cafés." He slid to the floor and leaned back against the doorway. She folded her arms and looked down at him, the purple red smears on her face at war with her eyes.

"My paintings were turmoils with one almost-defined image at their heart – maybe a dog fight in a Mexican market, or Leda & the Swan, or a Burmese hooker. Those are real examples. People were so grateful to recognise something, they deluded themselves into thinking it had been earned by all that paint and energy." He stared at his hands. "It was fake – I could make one in a day if I needed to."

She crouched down in front of him. "The boy whose fingers I am touching when I hold these paints – he was 'slick'?"

He reached for her hand. "No, he was good. Could have been good."

"So then," she said. "Why did you bring these old paints?"

She did not wait for his answer. "I will meet you for lunch she said, at *Marion's*."

She arrived at the bistro with the paint still on her face. She had bought three pre-primed canvases from the *marchand de couleurs*.

"We will start today, okay?" she said.

"We?"

"Yes, I will be still for you, and you will start to paint, and the angel who stood with us in the bathroom this morning will watch over your shoulder."

Before he could speak, she made a shushing noise and laid her finger on his lips. "I tell you," she said, "I know angels. If you do not know them it is a waste of your breath to talk about it."

"You're funny," he said.

"Sometimes funny is true."

Unfolding the brushes was like taking up something from the day before. His younger self had cleaned them well, at least. He sent her out for some thinner and leafed through the drawings he had made of her. It amazed him how many there were. He chose a full face portrait, and set one of the canvases vertically on the easel. She could sit to the right of the window, where the light would be constant. He got plates from the kitchen; he would work with the oil very thin, at first.

She sat by the window, with total patience till the daylight faded. There was not much to show for it, but he was happy. If this took a month, it would be all right.

"Okay," he said. "You were an angel. In *my* sense of the word! Shall we go out for a drink?"

She went to the bathroom, but came back out in the story shirt and sat on the couch.

"You haven't looked at the canvas," he said.

"I know it will be good." She patted the seat beside her. "You come now."

He went to clean his hands. He could not think of any story to tell her.

"I'm tired now," he said. "I'm tired and happy, and my head is empty."

"Just a small small story."

"You are eating up my life up," he laughed, "and you never tell me anything."

"So I will tell you my small story, then. Sit there on the floor."

He lay propped on his arm behind the easel. She drew the shirt tight round her neck, and began.

"You see, there was a woman who lived in a small, forgotten country. Her house was close by a town. It was really no more than a village.

When she was a child her mother left her with her grandparents. They had two cows and many hens, and they sold eggs and cream and butter at the market. And when her grandmother died, it was her job to look after her grandfather. She cooked and cleaned and churned the butter, and she could sew and knit also.

Then her grandfather died, and so she was on her own. And still she went to town with the eggs and the butter, and time went on.

Some people said she was simple, and perhaps she was. But perhaps she was very shy because she was alone all the time.

The bad day came when the partisans raided the town. They did the things that soldiers do, and they drove off the cows and killed all the pigs too.

The woman hid in the field until the sun was setting. She thought that the raiders were gone, but when she came back through the garden, she heard the hens carrying on in her henhouse. There was a soldier inside. He was snatching the chickens from their roosts and putting them into a sack.

She went in and pulled at his sleeve. You must not take them all, she said. You have to leave me something.

He looked around like a guilty boy, and then he threw her down on the floor of the henhouse and had his way with her.

When he was finished he began to weep. He was very young to be a soldier. She was the first woman he had been with, and he of course was the only man she had known.

He was homesick for his town in another forgotten country. He was scared of the fighting. All he wanted was to get home and go back to his studies.

It was almost dark. She lay staring at him, and he went away. He left her three chickens, and there was another sitting tight on her eggs in the corner.

She was not a young woman, but by the time the first snowfall covered the fields she knew that he had left her also with a child.

Well, she survived. And when the child was four-years-old, and strong enough to walk some distance, the mother set out towards the east. Mostly they walked. They went from town to town, and the mother took work where she could, sometimes for a day, sometimes for a month. Sometimes they slept in a room or a barn, and sometimes under a hedge. Sometimes people were kind to them, and sometimes they were not.

The mother was not a talker. She had told the girl all that she needed to know. Her father's first name, and the faraway river where his town was.

There were borders where there had been no borders. There were countries that no longer existed, and some with new names. In some places the language was different, in some it was the same.

They went towards the mountains. It was two years before they reached the river.

They stopped in every town there, sometimes for a day, sometimes for a week.

One day the mother saw him through the school window, with children all around him. She came back at day's end and followed him through the streets.

That evening she took the girl to his house. A woman came to the door with a child at her breast.

I am here to see your husband, the mother said.

He appeared from the back room.

The mother pushed the girl forward. This is your daughter, she said, I have done my share. And she walked away for ever.

They took the girl in. She had a little sister now, and a little brother soon after.

They never mistreated her, and perhaps she was not grateful enough for that.

When she was thirteen she went with some friends and stole from a church. There was an offering box by the statue of the Virgin, and they tipped it over and took out the coins and some paper money too.

But one of the friends got frightened and confessed to her parents.

So they were taken to court, and sent away to a prison. It was a prison for young people. It was in an old fortress above the river.

Her father would have nothing to do with her, but her stepmother came to see her one day. She brought a winter coat and some boots, and a cake she had baked. I feel ashamed, she told the girl. I did my best for you, but I could not love you in my heart.

The girls in the prison did the laundry for the police barracks, and worked in the garden inside the high wall. They slept in a long room where the light was always on.

They saw the boy prisoners at mealtimes only. Each morning the boys were marched down to the town, to work on the streets and the drains.

The wall went all round that place, except at the cliff top where the yew trees grew. No one had ever escaped from the prison, though there were stories of a boy long ago who had tried. He fell from the cliff to his death. People saw his ghost at the laundry window, staring in with a white, drowned face.

The girls would spend two years in the prison, and then they would go to a convent school in the city.

One morning the girl sneaked into the kitchen to steal some food. She found a back door left open. There was a terrace with tables and chairs, where the guards and their families sat sometimes. No one was there. The yew trees grew at the end of the terrace. She went into the trees and saw the river below her. It was very far down. She could hear it rushing against the cliff.

She was going to go back inside, but someone stopped her. There was a boy in the shadows of the yew trees. He beckoned to her and she followed him through the trees. She grew dizzy, but he reached out and took her hand. I will be your angel, he told her.

His hand was cold, but it was strong. They came to a place where the rock pushed out from the cliff. Now jump, he said. Don't look down, close your eyes and go quickly.

She jumped. He did not go with her, but she held his cold hand till the moment she hit the water.

The river took her away. It did not drown her, or beat her against the stones. It left her against a sand bank where willow trees reached over the water.

She crawled under the trees and slept there. When she woke, the sun was low and she set out towards it.

Mostly she walked. She went from town to town, and took work, or begged, or made friends with young girls on the street. Sometimes people were kind to her, and sometimes they were not.

She crossed many borders, sometimes in secret, sometimes by telling a story. For two years she worked in a town by the sea, and learned a new language. She worked on a ship, almost around the world. She went to school for a year. She lived with a boy who wrote music, and then she travelled with friends who played in a band.

They went from country to country, and one day, in an old old city, she walked along a street and saw a lonely man, with a foolish beard, whose hand was cold and strong and made beautiful things. So she went home with him, to be his angel, for a small time at least."

She opened the shirt on her nakedness.

"And here I am."

Her eyes were laughing. She nodded for him to speak.

"But you didn't once tell me what she was feeling."

"Of course that is for you to decide for yourself."

"Anyway," he said, "it's a wonderful story, but I don't believe a word of it."

She pulled the shirt close around her, and stood up. "Every word of it is true, all the same."

A short while after, she went out. He did not see her again for more than a week.

He set the portrait aside and started another, with her reflected in the hallway mirror, the estuary veins spreading out from between her breasts, caressing her throat, and her cheek bones, vanishing into her hair. He thinned the paint right down, and thought of his friend back home, with her egg tempera and minute brushstrokes, and the agony in her work. He loved the slowness of this, as though the image was there already, just needing to be lavished with care, instead of finding itself while the painting was in progress.

He gave it to her when she came back. "It'll take a long time to dry," he told her. "Be careful with it."

She took the painting without comment. Her hair had been cut very short, and in her jeans and leather boots she was boylike, and very young.

"I have been with someone else," she said. "Our small time is finished now."

She smelled like a different person when she kissed him goodbye.

He was sure that his heart must be broken, but all he did was work. He was in that space he remembered from years before, the trance of concentration. He used to promise himself that he'd notice the next time, and savour the magic consciously, but he never did.

He worked slowly and without pause, taking time just for a sandwich and drink in the evening, drinking coffee constantly. He woke after short, dreamless sleeps, with nothing but the portrait on his mind. A week went by, perhaps two. His face in the mirror was tired but alive every time he looked.

The portrait grew more and more real to him. It was as though all the shades of her were revealing themselves in this one expression, this minute tilt of her head. He loved the skin with his brush, and the paint ate up time. At the end he felt as though he was drawing paint from the surface, rather than applying it — that is how he got the eyes all at once to be startlingly hers. Was it finished? He'd see tomorrow.

He was utterly spent, but even as he almost crawled to his bed in the late afternoon, some part of his mind was thinking already about other pictures, other textures, other strokes.

He woke in the night to the sound of someone in the hallway, removing a coat and shoes. She came into the bedroom and he heard her undressing in the darkness, her clothes falling by the bed. She slid in beside him and pressed herself close. Her kisses were slow and exploring, her hands flowed over him. They had never made love like this before. He had forgotten what physical love could be.

She lay in his arms, her face close to his on the pillow. There was nothing to say.

He was almost asleep again when she got out of bed and went through to the main room. He saw the easel light come on, heard her breathing through there.

Then she was dressing again, a faint silhouette in the doorway. She leaned in. "It is finished," she said. "It is good."

It was still dark when he woke. It was cold, he must have left the window open. He got dressed and went slowly out. His face loomed in the mirror, lit by the easel lights, as he went through. She hadn't left; she was standing by the window at the edge of the light pool.

He crossed the room and she stepped into the light. He stared at his young wife's face.

She was barefoot, in a loose cotton dress. She came smiling to him and put her arms round his neck. She stood on tiptoe and kissed him.

"This must be a dream," he said aloud.

They were the same deep kisses as in the night.

"I'm exhausted I know," he said. "How could you still be so young?"

She kissed him again. "My darling, when you're dead, you don't ever have to change."

"You're not dead," he said.

"Oh yes, dear. You forget."

"No," he said, "you are not. You have a husband and children. You — "

"Children?" He saw doubt creeping into her eyes.

"They're almost grown up. You know that. You're happy, you have a career."

She stepped back and looked up at him, like a child being given terrible news.

He felt as though he was breaking her heart again.

"You're not dead, truly."

Her hands clutched each other. "Oh dear," she whispered. "Perhaps I have been mistaken."

He could only watch her, going slowly across the room, head bent, her hands clasped before her, taking small, unwilling steps. After a while he heard the door open, and close.

He wished that the sun was up. He wished that wedge heels were clipping along the sidewalks, and that the smell of bread was in the air and he could go out and mingle with the crowd.

He looked towards the easel. One disbelief replaced another.

The portrait showed him as no mirror or photograph could. The defiant honesty of it, the unkindness that was kind at the heart. The truth of it. Best of all that he had revealed himself without the technique, or even the materials, intruding. It was simply, complexly, him.

He wanted to touch it.

But as daylight slowly took over, and the smell of fresh bread began to creep in from the street, he just stood in the empty room and gazed back at himself.

Dibidalen

Among the discarded dialects of the Nordic hinterland was one that may even have been a language all of its own. Spoken only by young girls in two lakeside communes, it was passed on to each generation and abandoned in turn as childhood was left behind.

It is claimed that this language was never heard in the home, though it is hard to believe that two sisters, for instance, huddled together in their box bed behind the stove, would not have whispered in the speech of their daylight games.

And how could that language have truly been forgotten, as adolescence merged into womanhood? Did a mother, bending to kiss her daughter goodnight, never whisper something that would widen the girl's eyes in impish conspiracy? When women gathered at the stream to wash clothes or draw water, would a snatch of song or poetry never break out and set them all laughing, or singing together, recalling their innocence? For this was the language of the curious games they'd once played, as their daughters played still, with skeins of wool, and pocket stones, and a green rope plaited from willow bark, the language of the songs they had chanted as they sat in their rings below the Dibidil Falls, or ran through the open birch woods with the boy tribe's taunts at their backs.

The memory of those games and pursuits is preserved in four wartime letters sent to the Lutheran pastor of Gruenwald, in Judenberg. His sister's son served with a mountain brigade in the first northern strike, taking and later retaking the port city of Narvik, and pacifying the Kvener uplands; but in the tranquil second year of the occupation he found the leisure to indulge his uncle's passion for folklore and philology

In the first letter the young oberleutnant mentions an encounter with two elderly women. He had heard them quietly singing, as if to comfort each other, and when he asked an interpreter what the song might be he was told it was all nonsense, that the women talked only gibberish when they were alone. Yet when questioned, the older one understood and responded in the common tongue. "This might have intrigued you," he writes. "They come from a remote hill village where, who knows, a primitive form of the language may have survived."

It would seem that the pastor was indeed intrigued, for the second letter, written some three weeks later, details subsequent meetings with the women: "I have showed them small kindnesses that have earned me a measure of trust, though I am obliged to wear civilian clothes, as the sight of a uniform sends the younger crone into mute withdrawal."

The women shared two of their childhood songs, a few lines of which he transcribed by ear (they bear little resemblance, if any, to the modern Kvensk or Sami languages). They spoke of their childhoods, and the games they had played as young girls, endlessly harassed by the boys who were forbidden to join them. The boys, they said, had no secrets of their own and could not speak their *mussprak* as they called it (the young girls, apparently, were known as "mice," and the boys as *snamus*, "snow mice").

There were stories, too, folktales, "which they recount as if they were literal fact." A secretary was taking them down in shorthand, as the interpreter spoke, and would be typing them up for the uncle's benefit. "You would be so amused at the interpreter's indignations. *Why are you talking to these old fools? They are ignorant peasants. You want us to seem like primitives, subhuman, and hold us up to ridicule.* All the same, though his words to me verge upon insubordination, he takes more pains to be accurate here than in our usual interrogations. He treats the 'old fools' with respect and asks many questions. I believe he is secretly quite enchanted with their fairytales."

The only one of those stories to survive is contained in the fourth letter, which arrived in Gruenwald a few days after the writer's death in a roadside partisan ambush. It is typed on two sheets of coarse, wartime paper:

In the time before, when our valley, they say, was green every month of the year, there was a berry month too. Then the women went up to the fells to gather cloud-berries and lingons.

There was a man, they say, who went up with his bow and his spear to watch over the women. He was guarding them from the animals, from the bears and the wolves.

That man's name was Hermelin. He was a hunter who lived alone. His wife had died giving birth, and the child had died too.

So he walked about on the fells, among the women, with his bow and his spear. There was one there whose face he did not know. She was small and quick. She went on all fours among the bushes and she was picking cloudberries with her teeth. Yes, she bit off each berry and spat it into a basket that hung at her breast. A small green basket of willow bark, very cleverly made.

He watched that woman, and saw that she picked more berries than the others. She was very nimble. And each time her little basket was full she went away, and then she came back, to another place.

He watched her, and he thought that he would follow her.

So she filled her basket and got to her feet and went off from the berry flats. And she saw that he was following her.

She went this way and that way among the rocks and the bushes. She might have been fleeing, she might have been leading him on. He could hear her voice as she ran. She might have been weeping, she might have been laughing at him.

He was a hunter. He followed her under the cliffs.

There is a stone at the foot of the cliffs up there. And you can see, where the moss has not grown, that long ago people carved signs upon the stone. That is where he came up to her.

She took a cloudberry from her basket, and bit it in half, and gave him the other half to eat.

Her eyes were brown, and his eyes were blue.

She was Hiiri, who is the mother of us all.

She took his hand and led him around that stone, and they went through a crack in the cliff there, as narrow as a grass blade. That is what they say.

There was a great hall, and people everywhere, all dressed in bright furs. There was a king and a queen, seated on silver chairs, and Hiiri, they say, was the queen's own daughter. There was music and dancing, there was food and drink, and they welcomed Hermelin to that country.

They say that there were no shadows in that valley. They say that the sun and the moon shone together in the sky.

So that man Hermelin lived there a long time with her, and they had many daughters. And he forgot about his life before.

And they say that one day, as he was resting by a pool, he looked into the water and he saw that he was a mouse, not a man. He saw that the food he was eating was dry seeds and berries, and that all those people in their bright fur cloaks were only mice.

And he fled back out through that crack in the wall, as narrow as a spindle. He saw his shadow upon the earth. So he became a man again. His bow and his spear were lying by the stone, just as he'd left them. Then he saw the houses below him and he set off down the valley.

His children came crying after him, and Hiiri came crying after them. So they turned into people too. They followed him down to the village, and the snow from the mountains came down behind them. They say that it was the first snow ever to fall in our valley.

The people wondered at the woman and children he had brought back to his house. The young women came to that house, and Hiiri taught them the way to make baskets, the way we do now. She taught them the way to spin wool and to weave it, the way we do now.

When Spring came, she went with her children up to the birch woods every day. So the young girls followed them from the village. She taught them the words to her songs. She taught them the games that we play. She told them the secrets of the land without shadows.

But she wept every night, they say, for her home in the hills.

So one day when the women were gathering berries, up on the fells, she went away from them all and was never seen again.

But she comes to some people in their dreams. We know this.

They say there was only one commune then, at the head of the lake. So when Hiiri's children were grown, they took husbands. Then they brought them one by one to another place down the valley. That is where we lived until last year.

The letter itself remarks on the story's quaint phraseologies, which are transcribed literally, as requested, from the Kvensk and are themselves perhaps translations from the elusive *mussprak*. Other tales are promised, and possibly something more concrete.

"Since your last letter, our surly interpreter has quite changed his tune, and shows real enthusiasm for these researches. I think he is flattered by your enquiries (the more so, perhaps, because of your office, since these people practise a revivalist form of our Lutheranism). He has proposed an expedition in search of further material.

"Though the old women's village was destroyed in last year's campaign, he tells me that there is another settlement farther up their valley, and the old schoolteacher has confirmed that the two *kommune*, as they call them, had much in common and shared several family names.

"And so, my dear Uncle, your interests (which have already made my time in this backwater more agreeable) have now made a hunter out of me, in more ways than one!

"I have requisitioned a magnetophon from the propaganda unit. It is a brilliant invention, I think you will agree. I shall take the young girls of the village aside and see if this *mussprak* has any legitimacy beyond nonsense ditties and skipping rhymes.

"There is a further appeal to this expedition, however. The hills above Dibidalen are rich in wildlife – there are bears, wolves, lynx and of course the wild reindeer. I and some fellow officers (including Oberst Reinecke, who has shown himself well disposed towards me) are embarking on a *safari*, as they say in our former colonies. We leave tomorrow and should see great sport."

One can only guess what hands may have held that letter, a last bittersweet memento, before it was put to rest in the pastor's meticulous files, but it was the third letter, sixty years later, that sprang back to life in the white-gloved hands of a foreigner.

The chance footnote that had led him to this obscure cache in the Karl-Franzens archives no longer seemed like chance. He felt ambushed, almost, as though the very ancestors he'd been searching for had been lying in wait for him all along.

When his wife became ill, he had abandoned his fieldwork, declined all committee duties, and confined himself to teaching. He cycled the two miles each day to the university and came home again immediately after his classes. His diverse family roots had become his hobby, replacing his lifelong researches into Algonquin prehistory.

His maternal grandparents had emigrated as children from a valley on the Finnmark border, flooded some time ago by a hydro electric scheme. Like many new Canadians they had left their memories behind them, and like many of their grandchildren he wanted those memories back.

Now he was travelling with his own granddaughter, while her mother took over the care of his wife. The young girl's gaiety and fond tolerance of his ways made him feel somehow both old and young. She was more worldly and more innocent, too, than his own generation had been, or her mother's for that matter. Whatever was new to her she embraced, and he was learning to laugh with her at his own diffidence. Each afternoon she went off to explore on her own: those explorations, he knew, most often taking her to a sidewalk café to meet the eyes of young men and strike up fresh acquaintances. He envied her carelessness quite as much as he feared it.

He had shown her – so often it had felt as though she were showing him – Innsbruck, Salzburg and the Zillertal Valley, where again and again she'd insisted they stop, get out of the car and walk away from the highway. It seemed to him that he had reached the age where he was deadened to novelty – as though every bend in the road, or group of trees, every church or hillside village, any dip of the land, merely echoed what he already knew. But the girl made him notice – when she exclaimed at a patch of flowers, or the pattern of village rooflines, the old couple holding hands as they brought their cows through a gate, the smell of a lumberyard even, he knew that this was what Prospero must have felt, seeing the world – *Oh brave new world* – through his daughter's innocent eyes. The gift of this adventure was all hers.

They would see Vienna, then fly to Bruges to visit her father's family, but first he was allowing himself this day in Graz, at the archives. He was a thorough man.

The letters had been waiting for him at the special collections desk, each in its plastic slip-case, inside a Prussian blue folder. The young librarian had spoken in a whisper before leading him down to the reader's room, where two other researchers sat at separate long tables, each in a small pool of lamplight. The hush was as reverential as in a cathedral. The librarian switched on a green-shaded lamp for him, set down the folder and then waited until he had put on the light cotton gloves which came in their own plastic wrapping along with a folding magnifier. She bowed, and left him to his work.

His German was fluent, but as soon as he'd drawn the first letter from its cover he'd known this would be no easy read. The handwriting was immaculate, but the formal *Sütterlin* script which filled the small pages was more like a stern decorative pattern than a language. He laboured to decipher the words, even more elusive, in their unwavering parallel slant, through the magnifying glass. He wondered as much about the upbringing of the young man who wrote so perfectly, as he did about the contents; and the faint hints of cigar smoke that clung to the pages suggested the old pastor's study more than a commandeered office in occupied Norway.

He'd read on conscientiously, but the second letter left him weary and disappointed. He had hoped to find some small insight, at least – years of research had taught him, superstitious as it might seem, that stray references were never in fact incidental, but were often the clue to the labyrinth – yet he had taken no notes; there was nothing germane to his quest, not a single name even, of place or person, and he'd set the third letter aside unread. The typescript, visible through the fourth slip-case, promised less onerous reading.

The fairytale was a mere curiosity, though he did make a note of it for a colleague in the folklore department. He picked his way through the brief covering letter. It was a dutiful chore, until he read the last paragraph.

He could not have felt the irony of the final sentence, even if he had read it with care, but by the time he reached it his mind had gone travelling sixty years back, not to the Narvik headquarters or to the parsonage in Gruenwald, but to his grandparents' home in the Ottawa Valley where they'd visited every Christmas. Here was a name at last, Dibidalen, and it called out to him from his childhood.

It was a song, a silly rhyme that his grandmother sang with his sister as they whipped up the eggs and stirred in the grainy batter for the gingerbread men, the *piparkakut*, that would hang on the tree in the front room.

Dibidalen. That word had come like a refrain in the song, repeated three times – *Dibidalen*. Once (how old had he been then, six perhaps, seven?) he had come to the door of the kitchen, the women's domain, in search of his mother, and found her there singing as well. He remembered his sister's sly glance of triumph as she sang even louder, and the way his mother had laughed then, seeing him there, her little man in the doorway with his tears of frustration at being left out; and then the smell and the taste of the mixing bowl scrapings – his consolation prize, his own lesser triumph.

But Dibidalen. It was not the name of the flooded ancestral valley, but it was an actual place all the same. He said it aloud to himself and sensed movement across the room. Two lamplit faces were staring in disapproval.

"Entschuldigung," he excused himself, with a gesture towards the papers in front of him. The faces looked down again.

He would go out for some air, then come back refreshed and see if the third letter held anything for him after all. If only there had been a fifth letter, a sixth, an account of that *safari*, some family names and faces even . . .

Outside, he crossed a wide flagstone terrace, leaned on the parapet and looked down the town.

The river was almost invisible, so hemmed in by the old buildings that it seemed more like a canal. The blue, studded bulk of the Kunsthaus loomed among the brown-tiled rooftops. To him it resembled a huge, armoured larva, a woodlouse or sea slug, shouldering history aside, but his granddaughter of course thought it awesome, spectacular, and insisted that they should meet there when his work was done. She would be down there now on some riverbank patio, among friends already no doubt, animated and laughing, in love with the moment. Tonight he had a special treat planned for her: there was a *gasthaus* three miles back on the highway, renowned both for its cuisine and for a fusion of folk music and jazz that was apparently all the rage now. He had booked them a table beside the dance floor; she loved surprises.

It came to him then that he would very much like to smoke a cigar. It must have been the ghosts of the pastor's tobacco, breathing out from the letters, which put that in his mind. Normally a cigar was a Christmas treat only. Well, perhaps he would indulge himself when he had finished in the library; his granddaughter did not expect him till the end of the day, and he could sit in a café himself, and watch the passers-by and feel like a man of the world. It was a childish thought and he forgave himself for it, humming under his breath as he made his way back into the archive wing and down to the reading room.

Unlike the others, the third letter was clipped to the envelope it had come in, the Wehrmacht eagle obscuring the Fuhrer's profile on the purple stamp.

An old man had come to see him, a retired schoolmaster. His son was under suspicion, and he was eager to ingratiate himself.

When it emerged that his earliest posting had been upcountry, in the valley from which the old women were refugees, the young officer thought it might be diverting to have the three brought together. It was arranged, and though the women must have been older than the old man himself, he pretended at once to remember them, addressing them in an arch and scolding manner, wagging his finger at them to their evident bewilderment. His wits, the writer surmised, were a little turned, but, "He did in the end prove useful, however."

"He confirmed the existence of *mussprak,* berating the crones as though they were six-year-olds at the memory of their whisperings in class, their comments and disruptions with their *devil's lingo,* their covert taunting of the boys and of their teacher too, followed by smirking claims that they'd said nothing out of place.

He told me, by the way, that *snamus,* the snow mouse, is not a mouse at all, but the local word for a weasel, which fits better, of course, with the boys' 'mouse hunt' – the vengeful pursuit that they resumed the minute that school was dismissed.

"He is a sly, frightened old creature, with something of the buffoon about him. He suddenly declared that some of those girls were called mice with good reason. *Yes, there's one born in every litter,* he said. *Just ask these women. They'll tell you. It's only the girls, of course, little monsters!* And with that he pushed out his ears with his forefingers, and made his eyes bulge, accompanied by grotesque sniffing sounds through his teeth and nostrils.

"I could not tell," wrote the nephew, "whether the rascal was mocking me or tormenting the women (they covered their faces with their hands) or perhaps giving way to a creeping dementia, but I showed my displeasure at that nonsense and he made a quick exit.

"He was back, however, within the hour, pleading to talk with me again. *I know you were angered by my little performance* he said, when I came out to the vestibule, *but see – I spoke only the truth.*

"He thrust into my hand the photograph which you will find enclosed. *You might think those girls are sisters,* he said, *but they belong to quite different families.*

"You will see the three girls, all in the front row as befits their stature. Indeed they are practically identical. I questioned him further.

"It would seem there is a species of dwarfism endemic in these valleys, the consequence no doubt of long isolation and inbreeding. This may be of interest to you or if not, to our friend Kleinhaller with his practical researches in eugenics.

"In any case, I appropriated the photograph, somewhat to the old scoundrel's dismay, and it is for you to judge if it is of more than whimsical interest."

Spleenige interesse – there was nothing more to the letter than that after all. Still, he might entertain his granddaughter with the story. Perhaps he might suggest to her that the evanescent idioms and codes of her own generation were a modern day version of *mussprak*. It was a shame, though, that the photograph was missing, dispatched, perhaps, to the ominous Kleinhaller.

He prepared to clip the letter and envelope together and return them to their slip-case, when he realized that the envelope was not empty. The photograph was there after all.

It was a square, sepia-toned picture of children formally grouped before a log schoolhouse. He held it closer to the reading lamp. Through the small magnifying glass the faces of long ago students stared up at him, one by one.

He must have gasped, or made some kind of involuntary sound, for the other two readers in the basement room were staring at him again. This time he ignored them. He leaned back in his chair and sent out a terse prayer of gratitude to the young Nazi officer who had sent this his way.

A minute later he had replaced the letters in their folder, pushed back his chair and then, with a quick glance around, he slipped the photograph into the side pocket of his briefcase.

It was the most dishonest thing he had ever done, and even as he told himself that he would have copies made and return it to the archives with apologies for his oversight, he knew that he could easily have asked the archives to send him a photocopy, and that really he wanted to have it to himself for a few days. He envisioned the time and place where the picture was taken. The original was tangibly closer to the source.

His granddaughter did not expect him for another hour and a half. He left the university grounds and walked down through the narrow streets to the lower town. It was hard to imagine that anything essential had changed here since the pre-war days. He stopped at a tiny coffee shop with two outside tables, and bought postcards from the rack in the doorway. He ordered a coffee and schnapps, and a small fat local cigar, and sat as he had promised himself, watching the people, eavesdropping on passing snatches of conversation, and savouring the mild, almost juicy smoke of his cigar.

The postcards lay untouched by his glass. He took out the photograph and stared at it in the sunlight.

He knew exactly how his granddaughter would react when he showed it to her. Her eyes would turn slowly towards him, those blue, candid eyes, so like her own mother's at that age, and she would exclaim, "But it's my little Aunt, Grandpa. And look, there are three of her!"

And she'd be right. It was hard enough to believe that the diminutive girls on the grass, with their pale, alert faces, and dark eyes and feral ears, were not sisters, triplets even; but the real wonder of it was that any one of them could have stepped out of the picture and become his fiery niece, Karin.

Even now, as a wife and mother, she looked exactly the same.

She was famous for her boots. Italian, Spanish, French, they were her great indulgence before her marriage. They added an inch or two to her height, but that was not the point, for her. In boots, you strode. You were brisk, confident, enjoying yourself.

A stranger, seeing her in a bar among friends or crossing the bank floor towards her office, might think for a puzzled moment that she was a child where a child should not be; but if they caught her attention, her amused, direct gaze, the dark, intense, humorous eyes gave warning of the character and spirit inside her tiny, elegant frame. She unnerved some people, and enchanted others. She was used to getting her way.

She could tell in a heartbeat the weak from the strong, and the good from the bad too, although goodness and good risk, she'd learned, need not be the same thing at all. Still, she prided herself on not 'going by the book.' It was a small enough town that she was allowed some leeway. She would have demanded it anyway.

The young man who came to see her on her twenty-fifth birthday failed every criterion in the book. He had been travelling for three years and his job experience in that time consisted of farm and plantation work in Australia and New Guinea. He owned a 1968 three-quarter ton truck and two chainsaws, and he wanted to buy some land outside town. He did not have an account with her bank, or with any other. She sat across her desk from him, reading the application form he had taken all of five minutes to fill out.

It was a Friday morning, and the sidewalks along her street were adrift in cottonwood fluff. Aries was in the ascendant, and the wakened air of the prairie had invaded the town. At day's end she would meet with her sisters and a couple of friends to celebrate.

She looked up into eyes of a pale, acute blue that seemed made to stare out at horizons. They were at least as amused and challenging as her own.

She pushed the papers aside. "Did you seriously expect us to offer you a mortgage?"

"I'm asking for a loan, not a mortgage." His eyes did not leave hers. His voice was pleasant, matter of fact. "Lend me the money and I'll pay you back in five years; probably sooner."

There was no guile in that face, and no pleading either. It was a simple matter evidently, for him. She smiled, as gently as she could.

He looked down at his hands, and flexed them. They were strong, but not brutal. "Couldn't the land be its own collateral? It's worth far more than they're asking."

"That depends," she said, and took up a pen. It was out of the question, of course, but she would go through the motions. "You say twelve acres here. What's on this property?

His eyes were ready for hers, amused again. "Trees," he said.

"I meant buildings."

His laugh was a boy's. "There's a house," he said, "but you'd think it was worthless until I've worked on it."

"And the trees?"

"Five hundred and twenty three Colorado Spruce."

"You've counted them."

"They're a hundred and six years old, most of them."

Their eyes duelled for a moment. It was more like teasing.

"And you're planning to log them?"

He swung round in his chair, looking out through the glass door panel at the tellers' backs. "They're sad trees," he said, as if he were addressing someone else. "Not as sad as the trees in this town, but sorry enough. I'm going to restore them. That's what I do."

His application said 'tree surgeon,' though subtracting his travel years left precious small time for him to have practised a trade.

"Why did you call our trees sad?" she demanded.

He swung back to face her. "Trees aren't pets, or ornaments," he said quietly. "If you take something out of the wild, you have to give up something too."

She laughed in his face, and saw his startled, perplexed look. The blood rushed to her cheeks.

"It's okay," he said, "I quite often laugh at myself. But things can be true as well as silly." The strong hands flexed again. "My grandmother planted a tree, a sapling, for each of us when we were born. The faith in that's quite scary when you think about it, but she tended them like her own — they *were* her own — and they're still thriving. So are we.

"She's dead now," he said, "but she's in those trees, isn't she?"

For a moment she didn't realize it was an actual question. He waited.

"I see what you mean," she said.

He nodded. His lips were full — the lower one especially. Her eyes flittered over his features, his dark blond hair long enough, as hers was always, to cover the ears.

"You're an interesting person," she said. It felt lame, and she needed to bring things back to earth. "I wish we could help you."

He lifted his chin. His look, though, was level and friendly. "Okay," he said.

"You're the third bank I've tried, so I wasn't really expecting." He got to his feet and reached to shake her hand. "And thanks for listening," he said, before he let go.

As he went to the door, "Who planted your trees?" she asked.

"His name was Ivarr," he said. "Ivarr Bergstrom." He turned the door handle and stood looking down at her. "The trees have outlived him for thirty years and they're lonely for, well — "

"For surgery?"

That boy's laugh again. "There should be a better word for it," he said.

"Come and see me on Tuesday," she told him. "Bring all the details, the lot numbers, the clear-title owners, everything you can."

"Are you going to break the rules for me?"

"I'm promising nothing."

"Happy Birthday!" he murmured.

"Well thank you. But how did you know that?"

"Is it really?" He looked pleased, unsurprised. "That's what opal miners say when they find a real gem. On the mark, eh? Happy Birthday!" And before he closed the door, "You're very interesting yourself."

She tucked her legs under her, and opened a new file in the database. With the application form in her hand she watched him through the glass: his easy, rolling walk as he crossed the floor, the smiles he shared with the girls as he passed their desks.

She shook her head, with a smile of her own, and began entering his details. There was a double tap at the glass. He was there again. She nodded and he opened the door, leaning through.

"I didn't mean interesting because of your size," he said. "I spent the last three months among people as small as you are." He paused, looking at her, then laughed. "At first I felt really big and clumsy and pink; but mostly they made me feel smaller than they were."

She never blushed. This was the second time in an hour.

She was her sisters' darling. She had always been the power in their tribe, the maker of games, the instigator. They had families of their own now, all except her, but they still had their Friday night out every week. This one began with a meal at the *Poseidon*.

They were children again at these times, their birthdays falling at different times of the year, a party for every season. They were waiting for her, the waiters escorting her to the table, *Freshwater-Saltwater* twanging loud through the speakers. They'd bought boots for her, of course — red suede exquisites imported from Florence — and when a young waiter knelt to ease them onto her feet she was Cinderella among her beautiful sisters.

By the time they went on to meet up with friends at the bar, they were singing together, and through the evening their voices grew higher with every drink, calling out through the noise of the band in gay competition. Derisions of their husbands and parents. Highlights of their childhoods and teen years, embarrassments mostly. The wildest gossip from work. They were weeping with laughter. She told them about the man who wanted a loan to save some trees, and mimicked his earnestness: "If you take something out of the wild," she declaimed, finger wagging, "you have to give up something too." It seemed the funniest thing in the world, there in the bar, but in the early hours, lying in bed and replaying their night on the town, she felt herself flushing again, as though she'd betrayed something.

When he came in the next week, he brought the smell of oil and pine branches into her office. He was not a big man, but in the coarse grey jersey, down over his hips, and scarred work boots, he was a more rugged presence than she remembered.

"I see you're working already," she said.

"I'd better be," he laughed, "with that loan to start paying off." Then, "Sorry," he murmured. "I'm ever hopeful."

He watched her hands as she opened the envelope.

"You can sit," she said, but he stayed as he was, his hands on the chair back. She could feel his intense gaze as she read through the documents.

"Please don't break my heart," he said. She looked up. He was smiling, but uncertain as a child.

"Oh I wouldn't want to do that."

Neither spoke for ten heartbeats. It was not intended as suspense, least of all power — she was taken up in the moment, as she knew he was too; their so-different eyes looking into each other.

"Come with me," she said, and went ahead of him through the door, smelling the pine sap again, and his own man smell within that. He followed her as she marched across the marble floor, boots clipping, to the main counter.

She opened an account for him and authorized the loan.

"You're my angel," he said. The cashier raised an eyebrow and smiled. She went with him to the door, and held out her hand. He took it in both of his: "You should come out and see the place," he said. "Then you'll understand."

"That won't be necessary," she told him, thinking *You'll ask me again, and I'll go.* But four months passed before she saw him again.

There was a tight repayment schedule and she checked at the end of the first month. He'd been making deposits each week through an ATM. At this rate he'd have paid off his loan in less than two years.

She put him out of her mind.

She'd had no problem with boys, growing up. In a city this small, relationships were with people you'd always known. Adolescent passions were one thing, but since going away to university she'd learned a distrust of men. She could spot in their eyes that mixture of pity and speculative lust, and she'd meet it with a knowing contempt that would make them feel small. Perhaps she got a certain titillation from that. There'd been one experiment with a girlfriend that had ended in helpless laughter; otherwise she'd been celibate for almost five years.

Leo was in decline and the first skeins of geese were calling beyond the river. She came out of the bank on Friday afternoon, and he was standing there by the steps. His smile faded as he saw her reaction. She nodded curtly and was about to pass by.

"Wait, please," he said. She was on the second step; their faces were almost at the same level.

His eyes were so blue, and candid. "Are you offended that I'm being unprofessional," he said, "or are you hurt that I haven't been in touch until now?"

A dismissive retort died on her lips. She could not help what her eyes were saying.

"I've been so busy, and getting the house in shape," he said. "Now it's ready for you to come visit."

She imagined his strong hand upon her belly, and looked away.

"I'm meeting my sisters for a drink," she said. "You can join us if you like."

They approved. He had good stories of his travels, but they weren't about him, except in self mockery. She loved the faint accent, more a cadence, from his childhood in Wales. And he listened more than he spoke, interested in their lives, in what their stories might reveal about her.

He came back to her apartment. He was afraid to hurt her, she could tell, alarmed at first by the fierceness of her desire, then caught up in it, never once closing his eyes.

"Please come out to my place," he said. "I want you to wake up to it."

It was like a forest looming suddenly out of the prairie, the dark conifers closing round them as the lights of his truck wove down the narrow driveway.

In the morning she rode on his shoulders, clutching his strong neck between her thighs, yet feeling like a child, too, being carried on an adventure.

The spruce trees, in three ranks, surrounded the whole place. At the centre, near the house, was what remained of an orchard that he was restoring. Beside a row of caragana bushes, she saw feathery asparagus fern.

"That was a garden," she said.

"The ghost of a garden. You can bring it back to life if you want."

She didn't answer that, and he walked her through the whole property, conjuring up the Norwegian who had had this dream a century back, and telling her about the estates in Europe – the avenues of lindens planted for the benefit of great grandchildren. She did not know what a linden was, the word in his mouth like a lover's name.

They came back to the house and he set her down on the threshold. "The big room was three, originally," he told her. "I took out the walls and put in the big windows. Now it's waiting for you to choose the decor."

She went to the centre of the room, and looked around.

"You're very sure of yourself," she said.

He stood backlit in the doorway. "I'm sure of *us*," he said. "Please tell me if I'm wrong."

She stayed the next day, made love by the caraganas and under the sloping roof of the bedroom. That night she felt that his heart was beating in her breast.

Her sisters cornered him the next Friday. They scarcely knew each other, and now she was taking off to the middle of nowhere.

"It's only nine miles," he said.

"You're not from the prairies. Nine miles on a back road in winter can be a death trap."

He was a gypsy, he'd be off on a whim to see Machu Picchu, or Angkor Wat or the Silk Road, or Timbuktu or –

"If I was a gypsy, then the wheels have come off my vardo," he said. "I could never leave the grove."

One of them jabbed his chest. "And where does Karin fit into that?" she demanded.

"She's what made it inevitable."

They came round in time, of course, and often spent weekends in the grove with their children. They were the only company really, except for occasional people he'd met in his travels, who would stop for a day or two and give her a glimpse of the person he had been before her. Every one of them showed a fond envy – perhaps every gypsy was in search of his own forest clearing.

He was shy of praise, distrustful of it even from her, yet he needed it as much as any man, and she learned how and when she should give it. He was not humble either, beneath the surface. There was a core of certainty, even arrogance there; his gentleness was not weakness. He was someone who could trust his own instincts.

Her sisters could have warned him about her Furies. She was quick to anger, as she was to laughter and tenderness, but there were times of the month when she was a maenad. She'd suppress it at work, but then the rage would take fiercer hold, a ragged wind looting through her. When she'd lived alone she had found her own ways to survive, manically house cleaning until a weeping fit overcame her, or an erotic frenzy. Now, she would look back, each time in near disbelief, and see how she'd goaded him with accusations and insults, and bare minutes later had clung to him, weeping for comfort and release. At those times she'd cried out like a cat under the moon, wailing in grief and loneliness, consumed.

He never fought back, though sometimes he would go out and walk through the trees. But he adored her. He told her that he would find himself at work, saying her name out loud, or the pet name that he had for her. Repeating it in wonder at her presence in his life.

She came to love the place as much as he did, and she did restore the garden, and plant berry bushes like her grandmother's, and think of things growing as she assessed mortgages and investments at her office desk.

Then she was pregnant, and he was as fearful as glad. In the face of her doctor and her sisters, she was adamant. She would not consider a caesarean.

"I don't want you to die, Mouse," he said. "I don't want you to be hurt. Please, I'd be lost without you."

She showed him a photo of her great aunt Freya, uncannily like her even in the laughable clothes and hairstyle. "She was as small as me," she said, "and she had five sons, all home-born, and all of them still living."

Gemini was entering the midheaven, and the swallows were nesting for their fourth year in the roof of the woodshed, when their daughter was born.

The next night he dreamed that the child had fallen in the orchard, was lying with her face broken, dying. He was more changed by parenthood than his wife was. His nightmares replaced her madnesses, and awoke in her a doubly maternal side.

Now it was more often his daughter who rode on his shoulders as they walked the bounds of their little estate. It was his joy to read her the bedtime stories, and to say the last goodnight. He would find himself at work — halfway up an elm tree on a city street, or trimming low branches along a cemetery aisle — smiling at something she had said or done, or simply at the thought of her.

By the time she was four she had reached her mother's shoulders. His love for them both was the one protective charm that might keep them from harm. He'd dream of them vanishing, of crying out for them among the bare stones of a hillside. His wife's arms were more consolation, in his waking, than she could have guessed.

Taurus was in the eighth house, and the coyotes were clamouring each night, out beyond the trees, to the waxing moon.

She phoned from the city. She'd been shopping with her sisters and they'd run into some musicians, playing on the riverbank. One of them had a gig that night at a folk club, and they were going to hear him. "He's flying to Europe in the morning," she said. "I told him to come stay with us, and we'd take him to the airport. Why sleep in a crummy motel, don't you think?"

"Okay," he said. "Should I stay up, then?"

"No, he said they'd be done by about ten. He's a storyteller too, you'll really like him."

He did, too. The singer was older than he'd expected, in his forties at least, still footloose with just his guitar case and a canvas kit bag. He had a face that was made for shrewd laughter. "Karin says I have to wake up here to appreciate it," he said as they shook hands. "It's pretty atmospheric by moonlight anyway."

"We'll walk round it in the morning, before you leave."

He opened a bottle of wine, and she brought sandwiches out from the kitchen. They sat talking, sharing their stories by the open fire. The year before, the singer told them, he had found the love of his life. He laughed at his own words, and then shrugged — it was true. They were meeting in Italy and would spend the next two months, entirely free, exploring the back roads and planning their future.

There was a wail from upstairs, and the cry "Daddy, Daddy!"

"She has bad dreams sometimes."

"So does her father."

The child appeared on the stairs, and he carried her down to sit on his lap. "What was it, Sweetheart?"

"It was a scary dream," she said fiercely, and then started sobbing at the memory of it. "There was a giant, and he came out of the woods and he was chasing me down the field."

"You're safe now," her mother said. "It was only a dream, you know that, and you're here with us now."

"Did he say anything, your giant?" the singer asked.

They were startled by that. They shared a look of annoyance, and the child seemed to notice the singer for the first time. He kept the question in his face. She shook her head.

"I wonder if he was lonely," the singer said, with great seriousness. "I wonder if he wanted to say *Little human girl, please take me home with you. I would sleep in the woodshed, I would fetch and carry and work in the garden. If I could only, sometimes, for just a little while, sit and warm my hands at the fire.*"

The child stared, not sure of herself or of him, then buried her face in her father's shoulder.

The singer went to the door where his guitar case lay. He came back with the instrument, striking two light chords, and the child's eyes followed him. She lifted her head to watch as he sat on the hearth's edge.

His fingers moved over the strings, very softly. "It must be lonely, you know, for those giants and trolls and clumsy bogles. Imagine having to sleep under bushes or rocks or in a cold, draughty cave, when you can see the lights of a home, where people sleep safely under a roof and with a warm fire burning, like this one, and even the cat can come in and lie by the hearth, but you have to hide, so that no one ever sees you, because you're so shy."

The child's eyes moved from his face to his hands.

He began the story of a wild, timid creature, and a mountain valley where the cloudberries grow:

His hands are so cold
he comes blundering down
to the rim of the soft land

His fingers rippled like water over the strings, then became almost inaudible behind his words:

He follows the water
to the edge of his world
a shadow upon the cliff top, staring

He was half-talking but as the story went on, the notes and occasional soft harmonics made it into a song. He told how the creature steals down to a village where the houses are built out of mountain pines, and their roofs are thatched with reeds from the lakeside. The people are sleeping, and as their fires die down,

the small dreams settle
around the hearths

Poor Troll, he sang

Poor Troll he comes visiting again in the moonlight
afraid of dogs, of discovery, of breaking things

Sometimes he seemed to be singing to himself, or to the guitar as he leaned his face over the strings.

The little girl slid from her father's lap and leaned against his knee. He looked over at his wife. She had tucked her legs under her. Her lips were parted, her face as rapt as her daughter's. The troll stands by a woodpile, coming as close as he dares:

The cold light casts his hand across the shutters
clumsy and fearful

The thatch is alive, it stirs
like a shy animal's coat.
Like a nest of mice, the small dreams rouse and whimper

The child looked up at her father with a secret smile. The guitar made a plunging, confused sound:

He shrinks like a burnt child
stampeding back through the night

and she looked alarmed, but it was pretend alarm.

Poor Troll has come visiting again in the moonlight
He hugs the mountain
His hands are always cold.

The notes continued a minute, fading gradually until they were as quiet as the fire, though the fingers kept moving without even touching the strings.

"Poor Troll," the child whispered.

She turned and clambered back onto her father's lap.

"Bedtime?"

She gave a sleepy nod.

"Kiss Momma goodnight then."

Her mother came over, touching the singer's shoulder as she passed. "Thank you," she murmured. She and her daughter kissed, and rubbed noses, first with each other and then, in turn, with her husband.

As he carried the child upstairs, she reached back from his shoulder towards the singer. "You come too."

They stood in the little bedroom, by the dormer window. "Say goodnight to the moon," he told her, before he tucked her in. It was close to the half, just lifting above the trees. "You can't look up at the moon without being a child," he said.

The singer smiled. "I might use that line somewhere, someday."

"I'd be honoured," he said, and as they went downstairs, "It was magic, what you just did."

"Little human girl," the child called after them.

"It was a gift," the singer said. "To me, I mean. The magic came from your daughter."

"Anyway, I can't thank you enough."

She had made up a bed on the couch. "It's very comfortable, I promise."

"A couch by an open fire seems like heaven to me."

They left him sitting by the hearth, and went up hand in hand.

They lay for a while in silence. "Oh Mouse," he whispered, "I felt as though that song was intended for me." Her hand tightened upon his and she turned to him. He knew that in one way she was making love to the singer, and that in another way — through her — he was as well.

The flames had died down; the fire was mostly embers now, pulsing from red to orange, from orange to black, on their bed of white ashes. Like the fire in the song he'd just made, it was full of doorways:

there are caves in the banked up coals
where walls dissolve
and birds flash bright down the forest paths

He heard a love cry upstairs. There was bittersweet irony in what he'd given this household, when his own nightmares were unrelenting.

They were not dreams so much as torments that waylaid him at the tidelines of sleep, vivid beyond words. Each night and morning for the past two weeks, he had seen his true love drawn to another man's arms beside a dark, open window, while he watched from the door, intruding, humiliated.

He could not have imagined this ugliness in him, yet why would the angels send him such torments, unless they were true?

Two nights later, drinking wine by an ancient piazza, she shared what she could of the new love she had found.

He went out under the half moon, feeling unmoored from his shadow upon the cobblestones. There was something close to relief in his heart, even as it was breaking; the torments were not delusions. She came looking for him, and as they walked hand in hand down through the old streets, past churches and doorways that remembered far worse betrayals, he told her, "I'm on your side. This hurts me more than I could imagine, but truly I don't blame you."

"I cannot change who I am," she said. "I love you no less." And so it seemed, yet as she slept, still and peaceful beside him that night, he saw her again, pressed to a stranger's body, giving herself as she never had with him.

In the morning they picked up the rental car and drove north towards the mountains. Away from the highway, it was just as they had imagined – wooded valleys above each village, miniature worlds with wild hills beyond. It was perfect. They found the little town and climbed out of it, on a road that wound and switched back between dry stone walls, too narrow really for vehicle traffic.

"There it is," she exclaimed. "Look, look!" The *pensione* stood out against the hillside, its gables dark red above the long, open veranda. "Oh it's even better than the pictures." She rolled down the window and leaned out, oblivious to the tears that welled up behind his sunglasses.

They were shown to their rooms, and stepped out on a slender balcony. Beyond the hills the mountain snows caught the sunlight. The town was far below, just a pattern of roofs, brown and yellow. A cuckoo was calling somewhere close by, and the buds were opening on a great ash tree on the lawn. They would be here for ten days and by the time they left, its leaves would have changed the whole view.

Ash-tree, ash-tree,

he declaimed

That once wert so green!
Ash-tree, ash-tree!
What hast thou seen?

She laughed. "Not one of your better efforts."

"No," he said, "that's from an actual poem, by a man quite famous in his day."

She shook her head, smiling, as her eyes shifted towards the door. "The things you pull out of your vault!"

"I've given more of myself to you than to anyone else in my life," he said.

"Is that a rebuke?"

"It wasn't meant to be." But that was not true. Some part of him needed her happiness to feel tainted by his pain.

She went back into the room. When he came in, she was unpacking her clothes, hanging them in the closet, humming to herself.

He sat on the bed and began to weep silently. She closed her eyes, looking into herself, then came and sat beside him, leaning her head on his shoulder. A bumble bee came into the room, flew a slow circuit around them and out through the window. A car started up below, and moved off down the gravel drive. He turned towards her: *"Ae fond kiss and then we sever?"*

She laughed through her own tears. "You always have a quotation."

"It's who I am."

"It's one reason I'll always keep you in my heart."

Her portfolio was propped against the wall by the door. A fresh sticker had joined the array that charted her travels – a cliffside villa, and across the sky the name of that artists' retreat. Oh please, he thought, don't offer to show me anything. She loved to share her work with him, at every stage, but she was a realist, a recorder – she drew, literally, from actual experience, almost as it happened. This room, this bed, the balcony, the tree, the slump of his shoulders now – they might easily turn up, with her own curious slant, in her next show. He did not want to know what the portfolio held.

"Look," he said, "I'm going to go out for a walk. I'll scout around a bit; give you an hour to yourself."

She avoided his eyes. "Okay then."

The cuckoo was still calling, over and over. *The cuckoo now on every tree Mocks married men; for thus sings he . . .*

But it was a happy shout, too, as old as the language, *Lhude sing cuccu!* At every turn of the road as he climbed, his sorrow was belittled by what lay around him. Currents of warm, scented air flowed between the stone walls, all the airs of spring were insisting *Be light of heart.* There were meadows now on either side of the road, small tracts of farmland with a few sheep grazing, before the forest took over the hillside. He stopped to look down on the *pensione*, a doll's house from here. What was she doing in that room, what was she feeling? There was a Nahuatl poem, *Bean flower, black and white as the heart of a man who loves two women.* He had been that man himself more than once in his life, yet he could not imagine these two months together, with that new love tugging at her heart, another man's touch between them.

"Oh hell," he said, and with a shock of wings and a harsh, gabbling cry, a pheasant burst up from behind the wall. He watched its short flight, and then the long glide, almost skimming the ground, to the woods at the field's end. It felt like a sign; he climbed over the wall, and followed.

The whole valley revealed itself now. It could not have been more than five miles across, yet it formed a whole world under the sky. The Old World, with its so-different scale. Generations would have lived and died here without ever crossing those hills, yet he was as small and alone as in any wilderness back home. If he was trespassing, there was no one to see him.

A wall ran along the tree line but the forest had broken its bounds, and saplings were advancing into the pasture. The woods were lovely, and deep too, but they were not dark at all. This was the Greenwood, not the Wildwood, a beckoning of leaf-filtered light, and birdsong.

His fingers itched for his guitar. He could sense the words, lying in wait for him.

There was a gap in the wall. What had once been a cart track led into the forest. The wheel ruts were lush with grass, and young trees had sprung up between them, some shoulder high. *Weather and rain have undone it again And now you would never know There was once a road through the woods.*

It was like crossing a threshold, and he stood for a moment, looking out over the field, the way he had come. The town was invisible now, but something was drifting across the hillside above it. Was it an eagle? It was far too big at that distance. The sunlight caught it, and he saw the bright, pleated colours. A parachute, and then another, and behind that three more, floating down through the valley.

Sixty years before they would have been paratroopers, Luftwaffe fighters in their last ditch invasion. And he, looking out from the trees, could have been a partisan, standing in this exact spot. Ghosts upon ghosts, that was Europe; the air dense with them.

The woods drew him in. There was almost an indoors sense, the bird songs echoing, the air growing closer and drowsier as he pushed his way through. It felt ancient here, as though the trees were more than trees, hoarding human memories.

He could hear the birds, but not see them. And there were other sounds too, rustlings through dead leaves, sudden scrapings of bark. A rabbit appeared and went hopping ahead of him, unconcerned it seemed, but keeping its distance. He began singing to it, something that surfaced from his French class back in grade school.

Ah dites-moi, charmante bergère
N'avez vous pas vu le lapin, le lapin?
Si lui répondit elle . . .

In a fairytale, the rabbit would lead him deep into the forest and then transform into the bewitched maiden or, who knows, the wicked enchantress herself.

The track curved to the left, back towards the road. He would be out of the woods again soon. The rabbit stopped and sat upright, watching as he approached. He stepped carefully, holding his breath, till he was standing right over it. It looked up at him, steadily. "What's this?" he said, and it bolted off into the trees.

If he had not stopped, he'd have passed the house by without seeing it. Brambles and young trees crowded against the stained walls, and the roof was a mat of tendrils and vine leaves. The door had no handle; when he pushed, it opened inwards. The smell was unnameable – not mildew, not dust, the smell of silence.

There was one wide room, with bare floorboards, and doorways out to a balcony. A grape vine was stealing the light there, the leaf veins made shadow-patterns on the floor, and already there were clusters of tiny green grapes. He parted the leaves and saw the ground fall away; he was on the top floor. There were steps down to another balcony, and to four small rooms, two still with iron bedsteads. Another flight of steps and he was on the ground. There was a kitchen, a rusted wood stove and bundles of dusty herbs at the beams. Beside it, a narrow space, with a tin bath, and then a supporting pillar, where the vine's thick, contorted trunk began. The rest was a byre, the manger still full of old hay.

He stepped out in the overgrown yard, and looked up. Where had the people gone? What generations of Listeners had they left behind here?

He heard water through the trees and scrambled down. It was a narrow stream and a little way up was a waterfall with a pool below and trees leaning over. He cleared some fallen branches from a flat, mossy rock and sat where he knew many others had sat through the years.

The branches were dead and grey, with intricate white ciphers carved into them. He broke off a short piece, and turned it in his hands. His sister had called this elf writing when he was little, and it still was for him. He had no problem with contradictions. Elf letters were at least as real as the galleries of bark beetles. They both had their stories.

He threw the stick into the pool, and watched as it nudged towards the stream's outlet and swung round into the current. But almost at once it lodged up against a stone, and he felt the human urge to hurry nature along. It would not shift, and he stared till it went out of focus, and the water's voices closed in.

A man came out of the forest to a green valley. There was a hut beside the stream below, and the smell of wood smoke.

rap rap

rap rap

"Have you food for me, Auntie, and a bed to lie down in, for I'm lost and weary."

"Will you tend my fire, and never tire?"

"Aye, tomorrow I will."

"Will you stir my pot, and keep it hot?"

"Aye, tomorrow I will."

"Will you milk my goat, and comb her coat?"

"Aye, tomorrow I will."

Then stay and sleep, and here's bread and sweet milk for you. But when you wake, you must do as I've told."

So the man ate and stretched out by the fire, and as his eyes closed he heard her saying

Sleep your fill by the fire's side
Never wake till the knot's untied
That shall be at the hands of your bride

and she laid a string upon his face and his breast, and skipped out the door.

His eyes would not open, and his ears were sealed, and his limbs had grown heavy as stone, but his hands had life in them still. They took hold of the knot in the string, and it was a hard knot. It broke his nails and tore at his fingers, and each strand that he loosened made a struggle to tighten again, but his thumbs found their way at last into the knot's heart, and it fell apart.

His eyes opened, and he looked all around the room. He saw bridles and hides and a spinning wheel, and a great millstone by the hearth. There was a black pot hung over the fire and he could hear the brew in it seething.

flup flup

flup flup

Then a weasel came down from the chimney, and dipped its face into the pot.

"What's this?" the man said to himself.

Then the weasel's mate came down, and they both began drinking.

lap lap

lap lap

"What's this?" the man said out loud, and the weasels squealed when they saw him there, and one of them tumbled into the pot.

She cried and cried, and the sound wrung his heart. He got up and fished her out of the broth, and though his hand was scalded, all the thanks that he got was a fierce bite as he let her go.

He clapped his hand to his mouth, and with the taste of his blood he could hear the weasels speaking, and he saw clear through the walls of the house as though they weren't there at all.

"Begone, begone!" cried the weasel he had saved. "She's coming now, with the green girl."

He looked out at the hillside, and there was the old woman riding her goat, and a great girl beside her with leaves for hair, moss for a belt, roots for feet and bark for a pelt, and a mouth like a hungry bear.

The man ran to the door and out, and leaped the stream, and as he ran he heard the old woman wailing

Found and lost
Found and lost

He ran and ran, and a wind came up in the trees. It beat the branches across his face, and sang through the leaves

You should have stayed
You should have stayed
What shall we do with the green maid?

"It's all one to me," the man said, and ran on. "This is not my affair."

With that, he tripped on a root, and the leaves fell whispering around him where he lay.

She walks for ever now she's woken
The knot's untied, the promise broken
There'll be no peace in the woods

A jet plane growled overhead. He could see nothing through the branches, but the sound kept fading and resurging, it would not die out. He got to his feet. The stick had moved off downstream somewhere, and the story was broken. The gifts had their own flow and cadence, so hard to regain. But he would find a way to finish it.

He would write it down, too, though that was something he never did. Write it down, or record it perhaps. But he would send it to the little dreamer in the prairie grove, with her elfin mother and woodcutter father.

He had no idea of the time. He climbed back past the house and continued along the track, reciting the story into his memory, smiling at the refrains. Would the right ending find him, now that he knew his audience? He kept seeing that little girl's face, and her mother's across the room.

The track climbed a short distance, and came out into the open. Framed by the last trees was an old-fashioned swing set, strangely desolate at first: two swings hanging empty from their scaffold above the child-scuffed earth. Then he saw the chapel, and understood.

It was a miniature stone church, with arched, leaded windows, set back a few feet from the road. The door was locked, but he could see fresh flowers on the altar, and a votive light burning before a statuette of the Virgin.

The road turned sharply below him. The town lay in clear view from here; a few paces more and he'd probably see the *pensione*. He did not feel ready. He went back and sat on one of the swings, pushing off from the ground and lifting his feet, horizontal, in front of him. The children must play here, while their mothers prayed or arranged fresh flowers in the chapel. A memory came of his sister, arcing against the clouds, her head thrown back, chanting *Up in the air and over the wall Till I can see so wide* and daring him to climb on. That innocence.

And then, as the swing stopped, he thought of his beloved, down in the *pensione,* how she would see this. A man on a child's swing, his feet dragging at the earth, his hands on the chains, his head downcast. He could see himself, so clearly, in one of her paintings.

He stood abruptly and walked quickly on, down past the chapel.

He had not thought of her since he'd entered the woods, but there she was, all at once, on the road coming up towards him.

She saw him, and waved at the same moment that he did. Beside him, for a flickering instant, she saw a shadow, a troubled version of himself that ducked out of sight. She was sad for him, sorry, but she could not deny the gladness that she felt all through.

The affair had opened the world up for her, but she had no illusions. He wanted her, but she knew that would pass, as the passion that tugged at her now would too. If he hadn't been married, who knows? She'd just told him on the phone that she would not change her plans.

And now she was ready to explore and delight in this place, before her life moved on. Everything was alive here with springtime; there were flowers, birds, scents, even different clouds. These stone walls were worlds in themselves: mosses and ferns and atolls of lichen, when you stopped to look. She'd found a clump of wild pansies, his favourite flower, Heartsease he called them, and she'd picked one out. It was purple and yellow, with dark spots like eyes in a tiny face.

She waited for him to come down, and held out the flower. "To help heal your heart," she said, and saw him be brave, and believed they would be all right now, for the rest of this time. He would still be her sweetheart, she was sure, long after they'd parted.

They walked hand in hand back down towards the *pensione*. They would drive into town and eat, and drink wine, and be what they could for each other.

She'd looked forward to their laughter, their private language, even in these last two weeks.

An old man was scything in a patch of grass too small to be called a field. She had passed him and waved, coming up, and now they stopped and watched for a minute. "Just look at that face," her sweetheart whispered. "It's so innocent, almost half-witted, yet look at the grace of that old body, those beautiful wrists."

She squeezed his hand. "I think you're the one with a painter's eye, not me," she said. "I've thought that often."

"I make do with words, as you know," he said, and they set off again down the road.

The man called after them, a few seconds later. *"Ehilá, Venite!"* He was holding something up for them to see. *"Nido di topo,"* he called as they came close, and he gestured towards some rough steps in the wall.

It was small as a tennis ball. A perfect orb, woven from grass, with an entrance hole at the side. It was built round a thick stem of grass that the scythe had cut through. The man handed it to her. *"Vedi, all'interno."* It was almost weightless in her palm, and then she realised there was movement inside, and when she looked closely she smelled an uneasy musk breathing out from it. *"Ah, stai attento!"* the man warned, and knelt down at her feet. He scooped something out of the grass and held it up on his palm for her, smiling.

It was a minute, pink, naked thing, small as a nail moon yet alive and blindly turning. She felt revulsion in her belly and turned away, but the man took the nest from her and slipped the creature back through the hole.

He tugged at her sweetheart's sleeve and got him to kneel down beside him, and hold the nest steady. Then she watched as the work-blunted hands began tying the nest between two stalks of grass, a foot from the ground, slipping the stems through the ply of the nest with fastidious patience.

The two men shook hands. Her sweetheart glanced at her with such happiness in his eyes.

At the next bend in the road, she looked back. The old man was standing, silhouetted now on the hillside, sharpening his scythe.

He was crooning softly, keeping time with each stroke of the whetstone. *Topolina, Topolina, cosa fai nel mio giardino?*

In a little while he saw the grass twitching below the wall. *Toplina, Topolina.* Then her little snout came into the light. She sniffed around. She had found them. She stood on her back legs, and began to climb, so slowly that if he had not been watching he would never have noticed.

He put the whetstone back in his jacket, and turned to his work.

She could hear them calling, and the sound tugged the milk in her teats. There was the smell of humans around the nest, and inside it too, but the young ones were waiting, the nest was warm.

She settled in, curving around them as they searched for their milk. It did not take them long. Six feeding mouths kept time with her breathing. They were all one creature. She lay with her eyes half closed at the mouth of her nest, listening to the man's steady tread on the earth, and the voice of his scythe, whispering through the grass.

Acknowledgements

"Eggs in a Field" was first published as a limited edition chapbook, illustrated by Ryan Price, designed by Jason Dewinetz under the imprint of Wogibi Press.

An expanded version of "The Shark Mother" will be published in 2013 by Groundwood Books, illustrated by Javier Serrano and entitled *The Shadow Mother.*

"The Castaway," "Rendezvous," "The Shark Mother" and "The Doorway" are on an Earlits CD, recorded by the author and published by Rattling Books.

"The Shark Mother" and "The Doorway" were broadcast on CBC Radio Saskatchewan's *Sound Xchange*, produced by Kelly Jo Burke.

"Gramarye" was co-winner of the Carter V. Cooper Memorial Award, 2012, and appears in the CVC Anthology II (Exile Editions)

Several of these stories have appeared in *Exile* and *The Malahat Review.*

I'm grateful to the Canada Council for a grant towards the completion of this book, and also to the Saskatchewan Arts Board for their support on earlier projects, and for being on the side of the angels.

This book and I owe more to Elizabeth Philips than I can adequately express.